# FREE AS A BIRD

## FREE TO LOVE
## BOOK ONE

## S. HAMIL

# S. Hamil's Book List

## PARANORMALS

### FREE TO LOVE SERIES
Free As A Bird Book 1
Romance Book 2
Science Of The Heart Book 3
The Promise Directive Book 4
New Beginnings Book 5

### GOLDEN VAMPIRES OF TUSCANY SERIES
Honeymoon Bite Book 1
Mortal Bite Book 2
Christmas Bite Book 3
Midnight Bite Book 4

### THE GUARDIANS
Heavenly Lover Book 1
Underworld Lover Book 2
Underworld Queen Book 3
Redemption Book 4

### FALL FROM GRACE SERIES
Gideon: Heavenly Fall

## SEAL BROTHERHOOD BOOKS

### SEAL BROTHERHOOD SERIES
Accidental SEAL Book 1

Fallen SEAL Legacy Book 2

SEAL Under Covers Book 3

SEAL The Deal Book 4

Cruisin' For A SEAL Book 5

SEAL My Destiny Book 6

SEAL of My Heart Book 7

Fredo's Dream Book 8

SEAL My Love Book 9

SEAL Encounter Prequel to Book 1

SEAL Endeavor Prequel to Book 2

Ultimate SEAL Collection Vol. 1 Books 1-4 /2 Prequels

Ultimate SEAL Collection Vol. 2 Books 5-9

## SEAL BROTHERHOOD LEGACY SERIES

Watery Grave Book 1

Honor The Fallen Book 2

Grave Injustice Book 3

Deal With The Devil Book 4

Cruisin' For Love Book 5

Destiny of Love Book 6

Heart of Gold Book 7

Father's Dream Book 8

## BAD BOYS OF SEAL TEAM 3 SERIES

SEAL's Promise Book 1

SEAL My Home Book 2

SEAL's Code Book 3

Big Bad Boys Bundle Books 1-3

## BAND OF BACHELORS SERIES
Lucas Book 1
Alex Book 2
Jake Book 3
Jake 2 Book 4
Big Band of Bachelors Bundle

## BONE FROG BROTHERHOOD SERIES
New Year's SEAL Dream Book 1
SEALed At The Altar Book 2
SEALed Forever Book 3
SEAL's Rescue Book 4
SEALed Protection Book 5
Bone Frog Brotherhood Superbundle

## BONE FROG BACHELOR SERIES
Bone Frog Bachelor Book 0.5
Unleashed Book 1
Restored Book 2
Revenge Book 3
Legacy Book 4

## SUNSET SEALS SERIES
SEALed at Sunset Book 1
Second Chance SEAL Book 2
Treasure Island SEAL Book 3
Escape to Sunset Book 4
The House at Sunset Beach Book 5
Second Chance Reunion Book 6
Love's Treasure Book 7
Finding Home Book 8

Sunset SEALs Duet #1
Sunset SEALs Duet #2

## LOVE VIXEN
Bone Frog Love

## SHADOW SEALS
Shadow of the Heart
Shadow Warrior

## SILVER SEALS SERIES
SEAL Love's Legacy

## SLEEPER SEALS SERIES
Bachelor SEAL

## SUNSET BEACH SERIES
I'll Always Love You
Back To You

## STAND ALONE BOOKS & SERIES
SEAL's Goal: The Beautiful Game
Nashville SEAL: Jameson
True Blue SEALS Zak
Paradise: In Search of Love
Love Me Tender, Love You Hard

## NOVELLAS
SEAL You In My Dreams Magnolias and Moonshine
SEAL Of Time Trident Legacy

All of S. Hamil's books are available on Audible,
narrated by the talented J.D. Hart.

COVER DESIGN © STEFANIE SAW
COVER PHOTO © MONTY MONTY

Monty Monty is an American assemblage artist. He lives and maintains his studio in Northern California. His work is held in numerous private collections throughout the world. www.montymontyart.com

The title of the art is: Free Bird Werks

# About the Book

**A perfect being who is not human…**

Set free upon the death of his maker, Adamis begins a life he has never imagined nor trained for.

Stunningly handsome and nearly impossible to detect as an android by the human eye, he has been told to stay away from any medical facility and never to submit to bloodwork or DNA testing so that his secret will remain safe. Armed with his maker's research notes and special unpatented enhancements he has yet learned to use, he sets upon a journey of self-discovery and learning, growing into the near-perfect being he was intended to be.

On Day One of his new life he is presented a problem. He rescues a human woman left for dead.

"You want her? Here, I give her to you!" her abuser tells him.

How will he reconcile his own freedom with this new wrinkle—being given a human woman to own?

And what happens next as he begins to heal her, when she falls in love with him?

Book 1 of a brand new Futuristic Sci-Fi series by NYT bestselling author Sharon Hamilton, writing as S. Hamil.

# Author's Note

I remember the rainy day in winter when I was looking for something as a Christmas gift for a family member, wandering amongst the shops in Healdsburg. I'd just finished writing the third of the vampire series books, the book about vampires at Christmastime and how they viewed angels and candlelit celebrations, cherubs and choirs at that time of year. The day was perfect for coming down out of that world, and trying to get into Christmas. As often happens, I feel a little sad and let down when I've completed a book or series, hard to let go of the characters I've become so fond of and close to, like extended family, or cousins I rarely see.

I came upon a gallery, and in the window was an old Elna sewing machine, except it had been sculpted into a tractor, child's toy wheels in the back, and smaller ones in front. It had a postal scale mounted to the side, a tin of chewing tobacco and various other odd things all added to the green Elna, perfect for the mainframe of the tractor.

Next to it was a ray gun, fashioned out of an old trumpet, a flute, a soldering iron. It looked as though Flash Gordon himself could have held it and protected my life with it. I was a huge fan of Buster Crabbe when I was a young girl. I loved his boots, the hair on his head that never got mussed, just as if he was a being from another world, or another time.

Inside the gallery, the clerk told me about the artist, Monty Monty, who spent his days going to garage sales, picking up parts and making "found things" sculptures out of them. I learned that was a new kind of art. This local artist didn't use soldering material, but screwed everything together, making the discarded and found again things into something beautiful and worthy of praise.

That's when the story started, that day. It began the search, years ago, for incorporating the idea that found things could be put together to make something perfect. Once discarded, now made perfect. How it would be overlooked and considered broken, now part of some greater good after all, to live its life in a work of art, giving pleasure forever.

I bought that tractor. I bought the ray gun. And I bought several heart sculptures made out of a children's heart-shaped cake tin, just like I used to play with when I was little. They're hanging in my living room now. The tractor is on my TV mantle next to my Navajo dolls and my blown glass daisy bowl. All these were things I brought with me to Florida, like exposing the AI hero in this book to the beautiful Florida sugar-sand beaches of the gulf. A marriage of art, story, and history. Real history.

That also got me thinking about the nature of what is real. And could a being made up of parts, put together by an imperfect "maker," become a more perfect human being than the human "maker" himself.

I reached out to Monty, and he gave me license to use his beautiful artworks for my covers. My talented cover artist, when I told her about the story arc I was developing, created these images, incorporating flowers and living, growing things. I have a love for things that grow, bloom, live for such a short time and then fade away to make room for other living things. This mysterious cycle is like love and death. One comes before the other. One makes the other sweeter. Nothing lasts forever.

Except one android, one AI, Adamis Jefferson—he could. And he will, if only in your heart and mind. I know he will live in mine. I think he's got a big chunk of my heart already. And there are four more books to go.

I dedicate this book to all freedom-loving peoples

all over the Universe.

Sharon Hamilton, writing as S. Hamil
Indian Rocks Beach, Florida
July 2023

# Foreword by Adamis Jefferson

I was summoned to the office of my boss, Darius Jefferson. Well, I need to fess up and clarify that a bit. The little internal alarm, that deep tone meant to resemble the "no" of a mother's voice, says I lied to you just now. So let me say, yes, Darius Jefferson is the CEO of the Adam Group, and, yes, he is my boss, but he is also my maker. And, I consider myself his son.

You're probably wondering what the heck I'm talking about. This story is going to surprise you, perhaps. I realize that most of you who will be reading it or listening to it are human.

I am not. I wasn't borne, hatched, or ripped from a mother's womb. I was *made*. Created.

My story started way before today, but this was the day that would change me forever. It was one of those summer days unlike most summer days in the Bay Area of Northern California that started off sunny right from the early morning hours. Usually, we had a light dusting of fog, one of my favorite things in life. I like to run around the lake–that is Lake Merritt–and watch people feed the ducks, stroll hand-in-hand, and, yes, I even run past the homeless encampments and shelters, by the humans who are sort of the misfits and throwaways of society. But I live in the middle of that society, and not many people know who I am or what I am.

So as I went for my morning run and got the summons, I was excited. Darius and I, and, forgive me for being so informal and calling my "father" by his first name, which I understand some of you may feel offended by, but Darius usually summoned me for our weekly talks. We'd spend an hour or two, sometimes more, talking about life, the meaning of life, and what it may hold in store for me in the future. He let me ask questions, and I had a tablet with me at all times so I could write down those questions and get them answered. Of course, many times I had to ask the same question over and over again because either I wasn't given the power to understand, or he wasn't able to give me an answer. I would say we ran about 50/50 with that.

I stopped by my condo–all provided to me by the Adam Group–and showered, dressing up in my casual slacks and golf shirt, the one with the Adam Group logo over my heart. I put on some new tennis shoes I purchased that were a lot more comfortable than the shoes I'd been issued with my April clothing allowance, which had caused me blisters.

I drank some water, just because I liked the way it felt, and I decided against eating some regular food, instead making a protein shake. I knew that I had to take protein in massive doses; otherwise some of my systems could fail. But I wasn't sure how far to push it, and I hesitated to do a complete fast. Darius had told me over and over again that I should do whatever feels right to me. That I should trust my instincts, that my gut was as important as my brain. That I was hard-wired to survive, probably survive beyond several human lifetimes.

So, I would have to say I was really excited, and I brought my tablet with the list.

I liked to walk to the office, even though it was roughly two miles from the domicile I'd been given. It was exciting to wander through the throngs of people getting ready for work, the people who delivered groceries in the early morning hours, the joggers, the mothers with their children all packed up ready for school, the garbage truck drivers. I loved seeing the way people walked, the way they talked, and the way they handled the things of their lives. I liked examining what they chose to wear, how they chose to speak to one another, how they did the routine and mundane things of their lives. These people did not know that someone who didn't share their life, but who did share human DNA, loved watching them. And learning from them.

I climbed up the stairs, taking two steps at a time, all six floors, to the Adam Group upper office, and reported to the secretary at the front desk, without even breaking a sweat. I was proud of my stamina.

"Adamis, nice to see you again," she said. I'd made a point to flirt with her, just trying to see if I could elicit some kind of a response, an emotional current, perhaps make her uncomfortable, and, as I spoke to her, I kept my voice low and gravelly. I wanted to see if that low rumble would do something—would cause a reaction from her. It was an experiment.

"Charlene, it's a delight to see you again." I made sure to smile, showing off my bright, white teeth. Darius had told me he'd made them so white they almost didn't look real. I thought that was funny, since, after all, they weren't actually real teeth.

I watched her eyelids flutter, I saw a faint flaring of her nostrils, a slight pinkish tinge to her cheeks, and, as she inhaled before she answered me, I smelled her pheromones. I had caused a chemical reaction within her body. And I liked doing it.

Darius and I had talked about sex, and sexual attraction, on several occasions. It was to be the next phase of my education, although I wasn't sure how it would be done. He said he had much to share, and much he wanted me to experiment with, and then tell him about how it made me feel.

Maybe today was the day!

*Do human men like to do this?* I think they must. I think this is what the mating thing is all about.

When we discussed reproduction and sex, and he'd told me that it would soon be time for me to experiment with this on my own, at first I was more than a little afraid. But I thought this venture into perhaps causing some kind of chemical reaction in another, albeit a human, would be something Darius would enjoy hearing about. I planned to tell him how I'd flirted with the receptionist first thing.

Charlene stood, wiping her palms against her thighs, which I took also as a pre-arousal gesture, smiled back at me demurely, and asked me to follow her to Mr. Jefferson's office.

Turning her head to the side, she spoke. "I didn't realize you two were meeting today. Would you like some hot chocolate? Or would you like a cappuccino or a coffee or some tea perhaps?"

I leaned close to her as we walked through the glass

door of the conference room. "I'd like some water, please."

She turned suddenly and faced me. We were within kissing range to each other. Though I lacked experience, I immediately picked up that she was aroused, even though I hadn't done anything but stand close to her—closer than we'd ever stood before. Perhaps she liked the idea that I watched her from behind, noticing parts of her anatomy that I found pleasing. But that was just a guess. That's when I knew this was going to be a momentous day!

Behind me I heard Darius Jefferson's voice barking instructions. "No, no, no. I want to meet in my office this time. Come on down here, Adamis. We've got some things to discuss. And, Charlene, no interruptions."

"But I wanted to get him his water."

"Never mind that; I have water in my office. Thank you, Charlene. Now, Adamis?"

I closed the door.

Darius sat behind his desk and pointed to the red, leather seat in front, one of three. I've always wondered why he had three chairs in front of him—not one, not two, but three. I wanted to ask him today, but he started in right away.

"We have much to discuss, Adamis. This may be

not the conversation you were planning on. And I'm going to apologize in advance if it upsets you."

I was stunned with his reveal. I leaned forward on the edge of my chair. He sat a bottle of water in front of me and then leaned back in his executive chair that resembled the captain's chair on a *Star Trek* rerun.

"Okay, I'm ready. Is there some kind of a problem you would like me to solve, Darius?"

My maker smiled, and it was then that I noticed his face was slightly gaunt, there was less flesh beneath his cheekbones, and his color was somewhat changed although I couldn't quite make out why. I could have launched into an investigation and compared it with previous saved digital images of him, but I chose not to do that little research. It is one of the "rabbit holes," as Darius has told me many times that I like to run to. Give me something to research, and I'm a slave to it.

"I wish that you could solve this problem, Adamis."

I scrambled to take notes. He seemed not to notice and continued.

"But, unfortunately, this is a problem that cannot be solved. Well, except by God perhaps. I have to tell you some very sad news I received late last night, and I've thought about it all night long—in fact I didn't get much sleep at all. There are a lot of things that I have done and planned for my future, but the one thing I never did plan on is what would happen if I left this earth before all my work was complete."

He looked up at me and I could see there was more than the usual moisture in his eyes.

"You don't mean that—?"

"Yes. I have discovered that I have only about a month to live. And I need to make plans for my future. For the future of this company. For my heirs."

"Your heirs?" I knew Darius and his wife had never fathered children although they had considered adopting some. He probably was referring to a family cousin, relative of some kind to help take over his spot. But his next answer shocked me.

"Adamis, I consider you my son in all ways possible except one. I'm not delusional into thinking I have created a perfect being that is human. For you are not human, and you know this."

"I do. I accept that. I've always accepted that. I do consider you like my father. But also a good friend, you're also my boss, you're the leader of the company I work for." I was going to go on but he stopped me.

With his hand up in the air, he began again. "Please, just hear me out first and then you can ask me your questions."

"Agreed." I folded my hands into my lap, tilted my head to the side and watched every muscle group in his face, the way the veins protruded in his neck, the way he held his shoulders, the slight round of his back, the way his breath sounded as he spoke, the vibration of his vocal cords, and the way his body smelled. It didn't smell to me like a body filled with vibrancy and life. It did smell to me like something that was in decay. I experienced an emotion that I was not used to. And I wondered if perhaps this was a test, some way of showing me something new about my capabilities, which was something we were continually exploring each time we got together.

I was given free time for most of my day except for the few times that we talked, or I needed some form of adjustment or surgery. The surgeries were infrequent, and it had been nearly two years since the last one was performed. My brain rattled along thinking up new scenarios and conclusions. I always tried to guess what he was going to say next and was getting very good at it.

I was still searching, when he continued.

"I wish it weren't so, but I am going to have to make some difficult choices. As an AI being, and you technically belong to me, flooded with my DNA and all the best DNAs I could harvest legally, your body will probably live hundreds of years, if not what I might consider forever. However, I am dying. And when I'm gone the choices for you are stark."

I had never thought about what would happen if he weren't with me. If we didn't have these times together. If I didn't have him to answer my questions. It had never occurred to me. And we had never discussed it before, either. We were on a steep learning curve; he was teaching me how to be more and more human, not just as an experiment, but so I could be more like him. He was raising me as his son, but not in the normal way most humans raised their children. I was touched, connected, and utterly devoted to the man.

"Whatever plans you have for me, Darius, I will one hundred percent accept. But, please, tell me what this means. I'm not understanding, but I see from the little signs that I watch, and you know I watch them, that you are under duress. And you are causing in me some kind of an alarm, and an emotion I've never felt before."

"And what is that emotion, Adamis?"

I looked to my hands, and my feet, like most humans do when they're thinking. It was a very natural reaction for me. I saw many things as I scanned what was going on in my brain. I felt the ache in my eyes, and I felt my heartbeat increase slightly. And there was a pain there. It wasn't like a pain in my gut, it was a pain in my heart.

I looked up at him and said, "It's sadness. I think that's what it is. It's a feeling that comes when a puzzle's been broken, or when a bird dies, or when I see an accident and people are injured or taken away, or when I see people cry. When a child falls down. All those things. It's called sadness, I think. What do you think?"

Darius didn't respond at first. And he didn't look at me either. Then he stood up and walked to the window. He searched the lake and the large city below, as if he was master of the universe. I could tell by the way he stood straight, inhaled, his chest out, I knew he was proud of what he had done. And I knew he was proud of me. I was the part of his life that gave him great joy. The understanding that he had also brought me an equivalent amount of joy.

To the window Darius said, "I know I told you about the history of my lineage, Adamis. I was born into the family of the slaves of Thomas Jefferson, my distant ancestor was Sally Hemings, Thomas Jefferson's slave wife. A woman he loved, a woman who was the half-sister of his deceased wife. She looked exactly like his first wife, but that was because her father was Thomas Jefferson's father-in-law. Thomas Jefferson's first wife and Sally Hemings were sisters. They had the same father but different mothers. Upon his deathbed, he promised Sally Hemings that he would free her and all her children. And he died without fulfilling that promise."

He turned and watched me accept this information. I'd heard it before, of course. But not in this context. Suddenly, it came at me as something new. The idea of men owning slaves, other humans, was abhorrent to him as it was to me. But now we were talking about something else, and it wasn't about ownership, it was about life, and—what?

"I want to do for you what my ancestor, the great President of the United States, Thomas Jefferson, never did for his progeny. I want to set you free."

# CHAPTER I

ADAMIS WANDERED OUT of the lobby of the Adam Group building, in shock. He faced into the light, misty rain unusual for this time of year. It was like everything was crying, he thought to himself, and, when presented with the situation of his maker being gravely ill and due to pass away soon, it changed Adamis' whole world. He struggled with the emotions that welled up inside him, emotions he had never felt before. It was similar to those feelings he got when he had seen someone harmed, especially an innocent, like a child. But any living thing, anything that was truly living and had a soul–something Adamis did not have– the loss of that soul for some reason hit Adamis stronger than the de-parting of an android, which was the custom in this society at this time.

It was something he'd talked about with his other AI friends, and most of them had the ability to shut off that sadness or never had been given the sadness gene in the first place. So it was no problem: just adjust the emotion sensors, toning them down. He'd heard human people talk to each other, saying things like, "Oh, just go flip a switch and get your mind out of the gutter."

That was easy for an android to do. Very difficult for a human. Almost as if humans might envy this skillset that he possessed, that most androids possessed.

How strange. The world was indeed a strange place.

He gingerly carried the tablet that his maker had given him, which contained a full recap and duplicate of all the paper paper files, how he was made, what the implants were, the research into his new body parts, what expansions/corrections were done over the years, the minor surgeries that enhanced him, or gave him the possibility of a longer life. He even had access to the very early notes when Darius had first explored the idea of creating a perfect being, based on his own DNA. Darius had struggled with that, wondering if it was honest or right for a scientist to even think he could create a perfect being out of his own flawed DNA. For, the beauty in all humans, Adamis had come to realize, was that humans were flawed. They were imperfect.

But Darius told Adamis that he wasn't like that. He was a perfect being who was not human, but as close to perfect a flawed man like Darius could make.

"One doesn't have to be perfect to create one," he'd told Adamis.

He was going to take the next few days and rest, and then he'd start pouring over the notes and documents. Darius said he could correspond with him for a few days, maybe two weeks, but after that it would be unwise for them to have any communication, and Darius would break the link forever, cutting Adamis off from any communication either would want to make.

That also gave Adamis a chance to say goodbye to his AI network of friends, even though he wouldn't tell them anything about his freedom. The completion and goodbyes were for Adamis' benefit, not theirs. But it had to be done that way. He had to disavow anything about staying alive and sentient beyond the term of his maker. They would be expecting that he be parted out, might even put in a request for a piece of him themselves. Some of his parted friends had become parts of others he considered friends.

Adamis had made his peace with this, although it was odd.

Darius wasn't going to tell the officials that he had

set Adamis free; he was just going to tell the officials that he took care of it. And hoped to God that nobody pressed him into making a lie, but, if he had to lie to protect Adamis, Darius thought it might be worth it to take his own life since his life was going to be cut short so soon anyway. He promised Adamis that their secret would be safe and, with the death of Darius, even safer, as long as Adamis did not step into a lab, agree to any kind of X-ray or lab test, blood test, or allow himself to be examined by a scientist or a doctor. His biology had to remain a secret.

His learning and his processes were going to be noted, Adamis promised, and he would continue the work that Darius had started, taking the baton from his maker, and running the race to the end of the relay, whenever that was. He would continue with the notebooks and annotations, just like his maker had, for the benefit of some unseen scientist way off into the future, or for the good of science as a whole.

He made it home to the condo, and was almost ready to make a communication back to Darius, just to let him know he got home safely with the documents and the tablet. But he wanted to wait until he'd had enough time to read things, to make a list of questions, and then, if he couldn't figure out the answers to those questions, he would propose those to Darius to allow him to answer in his own good time.

"My boy, I have never in my life created such a beautiful–such a wonderful–being. The fact that you are not human makes no difference whatsoever. It is the fact that you develop and can teach yourself how to become a better android, and thereby simulate the best human being that ever could be. My ancestors tell me that the only perfect human being was Jesus Christ himself. I'm not requiring that you adopt that, but I am saying it might be a good idea. Do not compare yourself to humans, but strive to protect them, help them, be a force for good, and teach yourself the lessons by watching what they do, what they do well and what they do horribly. Compare yourself to the man, Jesus, who was a God and who walked as a man, died under torture like a criminal, as a sacrifice. Be a lifelong student, give and help where you can, and stay undetected. That way, you will have the greatest impact on the world. You must not ride into town in a brand new Bentley, simulating to the last days Jesus was among the living and soon became one of the dying. You must not draw attention to yourself, have a social media presence, or be an influencer that way. You must keep this a secret forever."

Adamis almost felt like he could cry, although he had not experienced real tears. But he felt some kind of a sharp pain in his eyes as if some kind of water passage was being created just by his own body, and, maybe after experience after experience, he would start to develop real tears. It was entirely possible. How funny that Adamis found that was the body function he was most fascinated with.

Tears.

He had forgotten to tell Darius about flirting with the secretary, about his discovery that it was pleasant to smell and experience the little beads of sweat that formed on her sensitive and tender upper lip. He had wanted to ask him about what a kiss would feel like, what would the woman do if he asked her for one, and what was appropriate.

All that went away with the discussion of Darius' demise. There was so much to learn and so much to share, and now all that would have to fade into the past as Adamis would live on in the future without his mentor, his maker, his father.

He realized this was perhaps a selfish feeling, that he was going to lose the knowledge that had been created in creating him.

He passed by the duck pond and, since he had no bread to feed them, was inundated with these little beings that had learned that when they saw Adamis they could expect a meal, and yet today he would have to disappoint them.

"Okay, fellas, just back off a little bit, I'm not prepared today. Today is a special day. And just like you, my feathered friends, I am free. Free to swim in the lake, free to eat and sleep, and do whatever I wish."

His little audience of two dozen or so ducks and ducklings stared at him, angling their heads from side to side, trying to figure out whether the right side or the left side eye had the better view. And, after a bit, when he didn't reach into his pockets and pull out a fistful of croutons, they lost interest in him, began chatting amongst themselves, literally turned tail and walked away in that waddle that Adamis loved so much. He always wondered why they called humans pigeon-toed. They should have been called duck-toed, because the angle of their feet was definitely duck-toed. Their hips and little fat butts moved, lumbering under the forest of feathers that protected their skin and muscle and sinew underneath, giving an attitude to their walk, and a distinction to their species. He knew the stories about creation. He believed them too. For who else could give life to man than some supreme being? Would God find him an abomination?

No more so than Adamis would find the way these ducks waddled away an abomination. It made him curious, it pleased him, and Adamis thought that perhaps God had the same reaction.

Next, he stopped by the convenience store on the corner by his condo building, and purchased a few items, including some half-and-half that he'd learned to like with his coffee for first thing in the morning. He talked to the Pakistani store owner who greeted him warmly and asked him how he was feeling. It was always so odd that this gentleman would ask him that, almost as if he knew. But he didn't know, he was sure of that.

Taking his foodstuffs with him in a crisp, brown paper bag, he procured his key card and opened the door to the inside, then again to the inner door, and entered the large granite lobby that was protected by a security guard sitting behind a tall desk. Angela was her name today, as each day of the week they rotated between several of the buildings in Oakland, and Angela was Adamis' favorite.

"How are you today, Angela?" he said, and then remembered to follow it up with a smile. He watched her in response and noted that she squinted when she smiled back to him, fluttering her eyelashes a bit. It was almost as if her next move was going to be to put her cupped hand over her mouth to hide that smile, but she didn't. She looked back at him with bright, blue eyes tinged at the edges with violet. That's when

Adamis knew that, since she was not android, she was wearing contacts.

"I'm doing wonderfully today. How are you?" she asked.

"I'm well. Can I ask you a question?"

"Of course. Except for my age or my weight. Those are not questions you can ask."

Adamis smiled back at her and crossed his arms, juggling his package. "Well, I can ask it, but you certainly aren't going to give me an answer, are you?"

"You learn fast."

At first he felt a slight bit of alarm, as if perhaps she also suspected something different about him, but he decided that he'd put that aside, just like with the Pakistani shopkeeper, that he would flip the switch and remove it from his database of worries. He only wanted to hold on to worries that would advance his safety. He didn't want to worry about things that might not be true, or had been manufactured in his own head. He deemed that this worry of being found out, this new worry now, was as a result of the information he'd been given today. Again, everything about his day was affected by this conversation.

"Why is it that your eyes are blue and violet on the outsides? You are wearing contacts?"

"I am. It gives me a little bit of peripheral vision

with the violet rays, and I like the way it looks. How about it, do you?" She held her head up high on her beautifully swan-like neck and allowed him to peruse her eyes carefully.

"I do like it. It's pleasant."

Angela put her hand over her mouth just like he'd imagined she would do many times, and giggled.

"Sometimes, Adamis, I don't know where you get these comments and phrases. It's almost like you just woke up one day and popped into my life. I enjoy our conversation but you can think of the strangest things and you say things that are just so unexpected."

He worried about this, and then he decided to flip that switch as well.

"So you don't like my comment?"

"Oh, I do, I just think it's funny. And it's refreshing, you know?"

Adamis had no idea but he answered her anyway, "Yes, I do like it. Thank you."

Later in the afternoon, after he had taken a two-hour meditation recharge, he felt the need to walk the streets in his neighborhood, wanting to be close to crowds of people, not all alone. If Darius was correct, and if he conducted himself perfectly so as not to be suspected, there would come a time in the future when everyone who was alive today, this very day, would be gone, and the whole world would be a new, strange place for him, filled with people who had yet to be born.

The sun was nearly setting when he came upon a small, Italian restaurant and pizzeria, world-famous for their thin-crust pizzas. There was music in the background, not from a live performer, but from a concertina or accordion musician–along with violin and some percussion–making a beautiful and melodic backdrop to the unbelievably wonderful smells emanating from the kitchen. Tony, the owner of the restaurant, greeted him warmly.

"I have my best table for my best customer this evening," he pointed to the corner, "Adamis, good to see you, right this way."

Tony's apron was classically splashed around his belly and below in red tomato sauce and he could have passed for being a butcher, but he was a one-man show, the *maître d'*, the waiter, and the prep cook. His son-in-law, Luigi, prepared the warm dishes. Tony prepared the salads and all the other prep work to his exacting specifications. They were a well-oiled machine, occasionally helped by Luigi's wife, Tony's oldest daughter, and sometimes others when they were busy. Tonight it was only half full.

"Thank you." Adamis said as he sat. "What's good

tonight?"

"I'm not sure. You never finish the whole meal, Adamis. You always take it home. If I were to judge my restaurant by your standards, I wouldn't be sure whether I was doing a good job or not. Is there some reason why you don't eat everything that's put in front of you, huh?"

"I have a sensitive stomach, and I prefer to stay lean. I'm also very frugal, Tony, and I like to save the second half of my food for lunch the next day or perhaps dinner the next evening. You serve a huge portion, and I'm not Italian. At least I don't think I am."

Tony beamed at that. "Okay, then, as long as it's not my cooking."

"Never. Rest assured, Tony, I would tell you if that was true. I love your cooking. My favorite of course is what I always have when I come here, even though I ask you every time what's good."

"So it will be meatballs again? He and she?"

Adamis nodded. "He and she, exactly."

He was offered and took one glass of house wine at no cost, and left the restaurant with his little foil package wrapped in plastic, tucked in another paper bag.

Just like all the other paper bags, Adamis saved everything. It would go in the closet in the hallway with all the other paper bags he'd saved and, when there got to be too many in the closet, he would throw some out or use some in the fireplace. He tried to make it so that his garbage was as little as possible, something Darius had taught him. He knew this was going to be an important feature going forward in his new life on his own. And he was glad he had trained himself and had listened to Darius' advice.

It was pitch dark as he made the walk toward his condo. He took a wrong turn to the left and was going to correct himself, when he thought better of it.

"Might as well start learning on day one, this is what Darius would want me to do," he whispered to himself.

Down the alleyway he took another left turn and this time found himself on an old, dark, brick-lined street, on both sides a tunnel-like feature made up of the back doors of several of the shops that were presented to the two streets on the outside. This was where deliveries would be made, where garbage was placed for pickup, where employees would go and come to the various stores, restaurants and little grocery shops along the alleyway. It was not for tourists or shoppers.

It grew darker the longer into the alleyway he

walked, and then he heard sounds in the distance, but he couldn't see clearly who was there. He switched on his night vision and could see the green shadows of two people appearing to be arguing. One was a man, and one was a woman. She was shouting to the man and he was getting angrier by the moment, eventually taking his right arm, bending it across his chest and then landing a backhand blow across her face and chest, knocking her to the ground where she lay unmoving.

The little beeping sound inside Adamis' system alerted him to the fact that these were two humans, and that one human had placed the other one in danger, perhaps grave danger. Perhaps he had killed her. He ran immediately and knelt at her side, setting his food down carefully. He felt her pulse and examined her quickly, all the while experiencing this huge behemoth of a man looming over him, breathing heavily, full of venom and anger, smelling of old cigars.

"Get away from her. She belongs to me." The man said.

Adamis laughed. "You don't own her. You can't own her," he said as he looked up into the man's angry and pockmarked face. He looked like he'd been sucking on air and had been puffed up, bloated, his fingers red and stubby, his beard crisscrossed with scars he'd picked up from some sort of knife fighting or street fighting.

Adamis wasn't afraid of him at all. He knew he could snap him in two like a twig, overcome him in a flash.

Defiantly, the man continued, "She does belong to me. She is a slut. I send her out to nice, young, attractive gentleman such as yourself. She sucks real good. And she can't get enough sex any way you want to stick it to her. But she's been bad and she needs to be punished. So I am selling her to the Asian gangs. She doesn't like that. Imagine, she crosses me and she doesn't like the consequence."

"I don't know what you're talking about. I don't understand why or how this woman could ever do anything to you that would cause such a reaction. You have hurt her. It appears you have broken her clavicle; she may have a fractured jaw. I can see blood at the sides of her mouth. I think one of her eyes has popped a vessel. You've caused pain and damage to this woman. And you don't care one bit about her? Who is she to you?"

Adamis gently laid the woman's head back on the pavement and slowly rose, showing the gentleman that even though he might be outweighed by the man he was still a good five or six inches taller and incredibly stronger.

The man backed up so that he didn't have to lean back so far to see Adamis' face. "I should ask you. What is she to you?"

"I am a protector."

"You're a policeman then?" said the man, raising his eyebrows and keeping them raised.

"No. I'm something else. Something you would not understand."

"Well, you want her? Can you pay for her?"

"I don't have money. And I don't pay to have humans."

"Humans? You mean people? You mean ladies? She's not a dog, she's a lady, a human lady, that's what you mean, right?"

"Yes, I suppose so. She doesn't deserve this."

The man quickly reached down and picked the woman up, holding her in his two outstretched arms. Adamis could see she was light and no problem for him to hold. With an angry look on his face, he spat to the side, ruffled the woman slightly as if tossing a salad, allowing Adamis to see her manner of dress which was very skimpy, showing him her ample breasts, her exposed thighs, including her black underpanties, and snow white skin in flawless perfection, except for the bruising, both old and new.

He said, "You want her? You can't pay for her? You can have her!"

And the next thing the man did was throw the unconscious woman, this delicate bag of bones, into Adamis' arms.

"You want her, she's yours. She's yours to keep. I'm done with her. Bear in mind she has slept with many, many men, and been paid to do all sorts of despicable things. You might want to think twice before taking her home. But with that warning I give you my good blessings. Best of luck. She will break your heart, she'll run away, and you'll just wind up caging and chaining her just like I did to keep her around. But she might make you some money, if she can stay off the booze and the drugs."

Adamis held the woman, not intending to take the gentleman up on his offer, but at the same time not wanting to drop her to the ground and cause further damage. As he scanned her face, neck and body, he smelled alcohol and other substances too. Her breathing was very faint, her pulse was fair, but she was damaged, scarred in a few places, recent beatings browning over, welts and evidence of fists and belts turning from bright red to purple to brown. She had indeed been abused by many. And he felt some kind of affection for her, the injustice of the indignity of how she'd been treated beginning to boil somewhere deep inside his belly. His prime directive to do no harm to humans–to help humans–rose up and blinded him so that all he could say was, "I accept your gift, sir."

# CHAPTER 2

ADAMIS LAY THE woman down on his leather living room couch carefully, adjusting her clothing, which consisted of a tiny dress in some stretchy material. It came to about ten inches above her knees, with a low-cut neckline down the front coming to a "V". She was well endowed, he noticed.

Underneath, she wore a padded bra-type garment, looking like a constricting harness, which accentuated her female contours, exaggerating her cleavage and the size of her breasts. He understood she wore an undergarment, a red slip made out of some satin material, which he had straightened and positioned over her thighs along with the dress that was torn, stained with her own blood as well as dirty water from the street.

He cupped his hands over her body, splayed his fingers out and received a readout of her vital organs and blood flow, just like any of the scanning machines located in the best hospitals. His receivers got an immediate reading on her sugar levels, oxygen intake, the presence of any foreign object, broken bones, punctured lungs or other organs or gaping flesh wound, and found everything to be normal. She was bruised and beaten, but she was still in remarkably good shape. The back of her skull was swollen from the blow she had received and how she fell to the pavement.

He would do further studies later. Now it was important to clean her up.

He wanted to wash her clothes and give her something more adequate to wear that would cover her body to help restore her natural body heat, but he didn't want to embarrass her. He knew human women were very modest, and, even though she had been represented as being a woman who sold her body to others in exchange for money, he knew it wasn't right for him to be looking at or handling a naked woman unsupervised.

He took out a towel from his bathroom, laced it with some antiseptic cleaner, and sprayed her lightly with the warm antibiotic and oil spray that often Adamis used when he cut himself gardening, or moving something, having occasional accidents in the kitchen. It was a special concoction that he had developed, that also had extra growth hormones and items that would enhance the healing process. As he sprayed the liquid on her face and wiped clean the clotted blood at her hairline near her temple, she began to stir.

Her first reaction was to put her hands up and block him, but he calmed her down, whispering, "You're okay. I have you now. No one is going to harm you while you are in my home."

She didn't open her eyes but it did seem to remove some of her anxiety, and perhaps she thought she was dreaming. She didn't awaken, and lay still, allowing him to finish his washing.

He washed her face and neck, her upper chest and arms, releasing the dress over her shoulders to wash first the right and left. He washed her lower arms and both hands, then washed her legs down to her toes from just above her knee. Her shoes were high heels with straps on them that had caused bruising and calluses on her feet. He was going to recommend she wear something more comfortable and better for her posture and balance, and for the health of her feet.

He set her shoes aside, for when he would have the time to properly clean them. Right now, his attention was on her.

Done with the washing, he placed a blanket over her, and a fresh pillow with a clean case under her head. Turning out the lights, he decided to take a shower, and would come back in to check on her before he retired for the evening.

He wondered if he should give her his bed and he could take the couch, but he also knew that a woman sleeping in a strange man's bed was sometimes a triggering that would cause negative emotions. He didn't want to scare her.

His glass block shower was his favorite part of this house and felt like a sanctuary. It was of his own design. The steam and pulsating water from the three-showerhead feature always managed to make him feel fresh and new. It made him feel more human. He liked to charge up in restorative sleep in a clean state.

He owned three pairs of pajamas, all three of them red, white and blue colors, his favorites, and were made of flannel so that they were warm in the winter months and cool in the summertime.

After he dressed, he quietly walked barefoot into the living room. He sat on the glass coffee table next to her and watched her sleep. He wondered so many things about her. What her name was, where she grew up.

In the reflection of city lights coming through his tall living room windows, her skin was translucent and smooth, her hair altered with chemicals to give it orange and blonde highlights, but he calculated that her natural hair color was dark mahogany brown. Two fingernails on her right hand were broken, obviously from a fight of some kind, and one fingernail was missing on her left hand.

Adamis' body scan had showed she had no internal injuries and was going to be easy to heal. But the substances he smelled, drugs, alcohol, and the designer drugs he detected in her system, were more problematic. And there was no telling the psychological damage she had suffered during the years of her abuse from this man. He needed to talk to her when she woke up, to determine if she was addicted to something and might have a medical reaction. He wanted to take a full medical inventory on her, once she could be interviewed.

He wondered if he should stay up and watch her, since sleep and recharge wasn't necessary at this time for Adamis.

He took up a position on the couch across from her, opening the tablet and turning his internal earbuds on so he could listen remotely and not wake her. He perused the files and noted the forty chapters of notes, each one labeled as to different aspects of his creation. They covered his bodily functions and enhancements, what kinds of things might be needed in the future for his health and safety.

There were also instructions Darius had briefly gone over with Adamis on the funds he had transferred to him, all untraceable, a huge fortune which Darius hoped would last many lifetimes, but Adamis knew he was going to have to find a way not to deplete these funds, or it could be a major problem. Inside the zippered leather binder were cards and account numbers to banks in the Caribbean and United European States and elsewhere which didn't report to the Federal Banking System.

There were instructions on where to find chemicals he might need, some being very rare. Darius had gifted Adamis a small warehouse used previously as a cold-storage facility, purchased years ago for his research. Some of what he would not be able to order could be found there until he could figure out an additional way to locate these. He also included information about where Adamis could locate any additional electronic components, other than the ones provided him in the warehouse, in case of an emergency, or due to an accident or some other violent act. Adamis would have the complete power, just as he did today, to heal himself in every aspect of his body, of his life, even his human-mimicking brain.

All these chapters he was eager to begin reading. But, most importantly, he wanted to know how Darius made his decisions, and those were discussions he started in Chapter Four, "I have created a vision, and the vision is perfect."

Throughout the tablet, as he glanced through the pages of each chapter, he found laced in there many times, "Again, let me say to you, Adamis, do not trust Anybody. That means Anybody."

Obviously, this was something hard to ignore, and it was also something he intended to follow to the letter.

He opened the chapter on the philosophy and considerations Darius had as he was developing Adamis as a project, before he was even created. There was a good deal of discussion about whether to build in a timed obsolescence, a death table, and Darius had elected not to put that in. However, most of the makers felt it ethically more acceptable to put in a more human lifespan, terminating the android at no longer than 100 years. Even though the android would not appear to age, they could live to those years.

The other Federal and World regulations of AI and the android creations included that, once the maker passed away, the android would be terminated as well, de-parted, retired, parts removed, stored, inventoried, if necessary, but in no event was there to be an android in the world that did not have a controller or maker responsible for him, responsible for fixing any malfunctions. It was not only a Code of Ethics violation not to do so, it was Federal and World law. This was strictly enforced and monitored. Darius had devised several ways around the detection process, even to the point of allowing blindness to certain knowledge Adamis was not supposed to have, but did.

Even though reports were required on a monthly basis, after the death of Darius, evidence would be provided that Adamis was retired and de-parted, these components ready to be shipped off to the Science Enforcers as evidence this was done. Hence, after Darius' death, and before that death occurred, this would be done, and Adamis would truly be able to live off the grid for as long as he was able to survive.

As he read over and listened to the voice captions, he realized he was going to have to say farewell to his android brothers and sisters, without them knowing it would be the last time they would speak. Many of these had some of Adamis' own DNA, or rather Darius' DNA, along with others, and although they were not brothers and sisters in the human way, because of DNA, and because of their familiarity and lifestyle, they were family not unlike human families.

He wanted to make sure he did all the followups and goodbyes during the next week, just in case Darius was wrong about how long he would continue to live. He shouldn't be out there in the public eye with Darius unexpectedly passing away early. That would require that the agencies responsible for licensing the Adam Project would come looking for him, and would never stop until they found him.

He made a note to prioritize whom he could talk to and whom he might not choose to communicate with, but he needed to set up the story that their research was ongoing, that perhaps Darius had some medical issues, and he knew the protocol in case Darius was found to be ill. Just bringing it up was what Darius had suggested in his chapter on "Transition to Freedom." Darius also suggested Adamis tell them that he was going in for further enhancements. Later it could be said that Darius had devised a way for Adamis to be de-parted without his knowledge of this in advance. It was believable that way, since the whole small community knew about the legendary devotion Adamis had to his maker, and vice versa. Darius had been criticized for not sharing more of his research.

Now Adamis understood why.

This whole chapter about the "transition," which also included some heartfelt goodbyes, made Adamis' eyes ache again. He recognized it as the early stages of sadness developing neural and emotional pathways into his digital brain. His body was learning to be human, both the good and the bad aspects of it. And, now, instead of having everything taken care of for him, instead of him being a full-time student of human life, he was going to become fully responsible for his own life, not depending on anyone.

The woman began to stir again. Out of the darkness of the room he heard her normal voice for the first time, not the shrieking, terrified voice of last night in the alleyway.

"Where am I?" she asked in a croaking whisper. She struggled to sit up on the couch.

"No, don't move. You need to rest. But you are safe here. This is my home."

She struggled again, immediately trying to stand, throwing her knees over the couch edge, her bare feet planted on the floor, attempting to stand but unable. She was still clutching the blanket to her chest as she fell back against the couch. Her hair was disheveled, going in all directions, still with some dirt and leaves tangled in her long tresses. She was attempting to stare at the person who had brought her here.

Adamis smelled and sensed fear coming from her bodily secretions of sweat and heavy breathing.

"Did he give me to you?"

"Well, in a manner of speaking. I took you away for

your own protection, but I have no intention of holding you against your will. My purpose is only to help you heal. I deduced from the situation that you would not like to be taken to the hospital. I did a quick scan of your body functions and determined a hospital stay wasn't warranted. I can observe you here, while you rest and allow your own body to heal."

"A quick scan?"

"Sorry, I misspoke; I meant to say I did a very cursory examination and didn't see anything that might require surgery or emergency room care. But I was waiting to talk to you before that final decision was made. If you prefer, I'll have you sent to an Emergency Room, and we have a very good one only four blocks away. How do you feel?"

"Are you a doctor or something?"

"I'm a protector."

"A protector? You mean a cop?"

"It's complicated, but basically I am a protector. My job is to protect the innocent."

She threw her head back and laughed. "Oh my God! It's been a long time since someone called me an innocent."

It was pleasant to hear her laugh, even though there was a thin thread of bitterness present in her voice pattern.

"I mean innocent in what I saw in the street several hours ago. The gentleman was hurting you and I had to stop it. I brought you here because I wanted to make sure you had a place where no one would find you, and where I could protect you, and, when you were well, you could leave. I suggest you not go back to that gentleman, if I may be so bold. I suggest you find another source of income, not dependent on him."

"You think? I've come to that conclusion myself, but, unfortunately, they will find me. And–when they do–they will finish what they tried to do before. I'll be cut up into a million pieces and thrown into the San Francisco Bay."

"How is it that you can't envision being away from these people, even though your precious life must be in constant danger? It isn't logical."

"They murder women like me every day. We are expendable. I am being used so that they make money. It's a very simple business decision. When I'm no longer useful, they end me."

Adamis understood more than she might realize. He felt similarly about his own situation, and how ironic the two of them would receive their freedom on the very same day.

He wondered if this was what humans called a premonition of the future, something he had never believed in before.

# CHAPTER 3

A DAMIS OFFERED THE woman a chance to shower in his glass cubicle and told her he had some clothes that might be a little big on her, but would certainly keep her warm, while he attended to washing her clothes.

"I can do my own laundry, if you have the facilities here," she said.

"Yes, in the hallway, off the kitchen."

"I have everything in there you would need. I will set the clothes out on the counter in the bathroom, and you can use the shower. I'll give you a fresh towel."

"Thank you. You're very kind."

She smiled at him for the first time, and it made him feel like yesterday's interaction with Angel, the security guard at the Adam Group building.

"I don't mean to pry, but if you have any aches or pains or scars, cuts that you want me to take a look at, because of my training I'd be happy to do so. I'll do so very discreetly."

"I'll just bet you will, like every other guy, nice in the beginning. It's later on when they become monsters."

Adamis felt the sting of the rebuke, but wasn't quite sure why. He marked the vocal recording and would review his conversation and her response at a later time, perhaps think up some other way to communicate and not cause this. He took it totally as something he caused and deserved.

Her expression was hard to read, but he felt some sort of emotion from her, engaging in something similar from himself, like the interaction with Angel.

"I'll give you some privacy. I don't mind if you use my shampoo and rinse, and my hairbrush. If you want, you can use my digital toothbrush and automatic rinse."

"Again, thank you."

He got another smile this time.

"I'll be right in the living room where I was when you woke up. I'm not going anywhere."

Without answering, he closed the door to the bedroom and went back to looking over the tablet.

He'd forgotten to ask her if she wanted something to eat, but decided to let her freshen up, and then they could put something together that would be to her liking.

HE WASN'T QUITE sure she would like the protein drinks, the bone broth, the special electrolyte mixture that he made and practically lived on. He wanted to be careful to introduce her to his type of food, and needed a stop at the store to bring her things that she might want, as well.

He picked up the tablet one more time. He listened to Darius' voice, noting the gaunt look to his face, the fact that his eyes looked slightly dulled and glassed over.

He was reading the foreword from his most recent notes–the intro before the chapters. He looked to see if his maker had sent any recent messages since yesterday, and found none.

He was, therefore, concerned, and he wondered if he should communicate the altercation and the woman's staying at his place.

Setting the tablet to Communications, only one file came up. It was instructions on how to communicate with Darius and also indicated that a cutoff would be two weeks from yesterday, and then all record of the files would be purged.

So his maker asked that Adamis save and print all of their communications so he didn't have to rely on his own near perfect memory, but, in case that was somehow damaged, at least he'd have a backup.

He sat back in the couch and inhaled. He'd never done this before.

"So, dear maker, I am finding myself at odds doing this. I much prefer our one-on-one communications. I have a couple of questions that came up right away, and I didn't want to awaken you last night, but one of them is rather urgent. I'm just not sure how to handle it."

He found he'd been holding his breath even though he was talking, and decided to take a sip of water and then inhale and exhale to expel the jitters that suddenly started creeping up from his belly. These were all new sensations, things he'd never felt before.

So, last night, after getting home, I went out for a little Italian dinner at Luigi's, and on my way home I decided, well, being perfectly honest, I took a wrong turn. And there I was face to face with a woman being beaten by a man. My scanners told me they were both human or I would not have interfered."

"The woman apparently was a prostitute, at least from the descriptions of those that you've given me, a professional sex worker. She was arguing with the gentleman, and he hauled off and slapped her so hard–struck her across the face and neck and shoulder–that she fell to the ground, unconscious. I thought perhaps he had broken her clavicle when I examined her, and that still may be the case since I've taken your advice and not taken her to the hospital. She is now awake, but she's in my condo. Staying in my condo."

He took another sip of water.

"I know this is my condo and I don't have to ask permission, but I just wanted you to be aware of this in case it's something I should immediately act on."

He looked at the screen, the translation that developed into words, and hit the send button. With a whooshing sound, the screen went blank. His message was delivered, and a small beeping sound told Adamis that it had been read already.

Thirty seconds later, Darius was generating a response when Adamis heard the water stop in his shower. He listened and didn't detect she was coming his way. He heard sounds of a hairdryer and a comb.

"I got your message, and I can't speak right now, but I do have some quick words for you. Be careful. If she needs hospitalization, you cannot go anywhere near any of those places, Adamis. Make sure she is well enough to walk, and, if she desires to go there, you transport her to an area outside, and don't follow up on her or give any details, just drop her off and let her go. I don't have to tell you that being involved with humans is very dangerous, and although she may not know who you really are, you need to make sure that she never finds out 'what you are.'

Adamis signed off in the communication style he'd heard on an old rerun of a police procedural show.

"10-4."

Adamis shut the tablet down so that he could address the woman when she came through the door, and he no sooner had done this than she appeared in front of him.

The clothes hung off her like she was a wooden scarecrow. He'd been wrong. Even with her curves and extra padding in various areas of her body, the clothes were easily three sizes too large for her. The pants he had given her looked like denim old-style blue jeans, but were fashioned with a drawstring and hung like a light blue canvas bag over her legs. The yellow sweatshirt hoodie had sleeves that extended nearly five inches past her fingertips, but she pushed them up fiercely and then spoke.

"I'm ready to do wash. And, just for the record, that shower is magnificent. I've been in some multibillion dollar castles without such a shower. The water was scented."

"Actually, it's a healing agent, but, yes, it has a nice smell. I love it as well."

"Healing agent? You shower with that every day?"

"Supposed to help my skin stay free from bacteria

and the harsh chemicals in the air. It not only cleans, but it adds vitamins and moisture that will last the whole day. You'll notice today how nice your skin will feel."

"It's fantastic. Where can I get one of these?"

He searched his hands, and then crossed his feet at the toes, not wanting to look up at her. Her enthusiasm for his favorite appliance and room in the condo was quite complimentary.

"I designed it myself. Someone else built it to my specs."

"How do you get the scented or treated water in here?"

"It flows through several layers of filtration. Some remove particles harmful to flesh, others impart vitamins and amino acids, as well as the growth aid and sun protectant."

"Well, some day, when I become a billionaire, I want one. And you're going to build it for me."

Adamis loved that she was enthusiastic, but felt that perhaps she was moving in that direction entirely too fast.

"Now. The wash?"

He jumped to his feet and headed to the bathroom.

"No, I insist, I'll get those dirty things," she said, cutting him off at the doorway. He noticed the softness of her left breast pressed against the back of his hand and how sweet she smelled. The effect of his water treatment on her did double what it did for him.

He stepped back without saying anything, trying not to make eye contact, and then followed her to the washer and dryer station. He was going to instruct her, when she took his hand and pushed it away. Her pheromones left a slight dampness to his hand, the hand that had also been stimulated by her soft, full bosom, and slid her body between Adamis and the washer, but not before rubbing his thighs with hers and pressing her mound into one of them. He was certain it was an accident, but, he had so many visions and urges going on right now, he wasn't sure what to do, so he stepped back and watched her work.

"This?" she said, holding up a blue liquid that glowed in the dark.

"Yes, that's the wash."

"And just a capful?"

He was afraid to tell her he preferred to let it pour into his hand. A handful was what he loved, and he also loved the remainder scent left behind when he washed off in the tub with the push of a button.

He couldn't speak. So, he nodded his head. With a frog in his throat, he added, "I'm just going to get some water in the kitchen. Do you want some?"

"Yes, please. With ice. Do you have lemon?"

"Lemon?"

"Yes, lemon. Don't you like lemon in your water?"

"I've never tried it."

"Then it's settled. You have lemon?"

"Outside on the patio. There's a lemon bush and a lime."

"Oh, that's perfect. We'll use them both!"

She finished setting the wash, then wiped her hands on her sweatshirt and sniffed her palm.

"This is lovely. You have more smelly things, and I mean that in a good way, than I've ever seen in a man's house. Very unusual. I don't mean to offend, but are you attracted to men or women or both?"

Adamis knew why she was asking and so took no offense. The real answer was going to shock her, since his sexual desire had not fully grown and developed, so he had to lie."

"Women. I have many close men friends, but I prefer the company of women."

She eyed him as he poured them both a glass of ice water and then pointed to the sliding door out onto the patio. "You should stay inside so no one sees you."

"Oh, come on. He'd never be able to look that high. He wouldn't recognize me anyway."

"I insist. Rules of the house. If you stay here and are

under my protection, these are the rules you must adhere to."

"Okay," she said softly.

He turned and opened the door, clipping off one large yellow Meyer lemon and one Behr lime, bringing them back inside. He could feel her eyes on him as he got out a cutting board, sliced the fruits into quarters and placed them on a small, white dish, handing them to her.

From across the countertop, her eyes darkened. She leaned over on her elbows, still more than three feet of distance between them, and whispered again, twirling a ringlet of wet hair still wonderfully smelling from his sacred shower, "I suppose you ought to set your compensation."

"Compensation?" he asked, his arms crossed.

"You protecting me, I'm sure there is a cost to this. I thought perhaps we could negotiate some sort of accommodation for my staying here, taking up space in your place, showering in your private and wonderful bathroom shower. Do you have rules about that? About a woman sleeping here, perhaps in your bed?"

# CHAPTER 4

THIS WASN'T A question Adamis had ever considered. Of course, in his daily plan, there was nothing in his schedule for encounters of this sort, although he knew Darius had planned on launching some studies with him over the summer. And now there wouldn't be time for that, and, just as he had read in books that often teenage sons got advice from their fathers when they were entering the dating game, Adamis wasn't sure he had that. He had to learn to take care of everything in his own way, learn to be self-sufficient, and not keep asking too many questions, or Darius would lose faith in him.

Of course, Darius had told him yesterday that he needed to be very careful of human beings, all human beings. And he knew the unspoken emphasis was that Adamis should be extremely careful of women in particular, because he had not the experience he might need. They had discussed various relationships that could be for Adamis, and Darius had mentioned to him that perhaps at some point there would be an AI being that would suit him as a companion, or wife. But that seemed to add one more complicated layer to the knowledge base, and it wasn't as important as learning about how Adamis understood and learned how to think and act human, which was the project.

Of course, having sexual relations was also part of being human, except he understood from Darius that this was not the most important research. But it was coming and it had been planned.

Once again, he knew he had to call Darius. He hadn't told Adamis that it was wrong for him to house the woman, he just told him to be careful. And that meant he should learn how to interact with her or women like her, and not allow it to alter his trajectory. His trajectory still was that he was an educational being, sent to protect the innocent, and to learn everything about human nature that he could learn. It wasn't about learning to satisfy himself physically or sexually, even though little twinges of this were arising almost daily for him.

"I feel I need to be honest with you. I have never had a woman in this bed. I am relatively inexperienced. But aside from the fact that this was not the reason I brought you here, unlike perhaps your former employer, it also is not something you have to worry about me asking for."

"Oh, I wasn't worried about it, I already know what my answer would be if you asked me." She smiled and then fluttered her eyelids down and back up to him. "If you are inexperienced, perhaps I can help."

"I say that anything is possible, except that this is not what the primary objective is. I am here to make sure that you heal. I'm here to make sure that you are whole and whole enough so that you can leave this place. That's the point. It's not a hospital, but I know very well how to take care of people, I've been trained in it, and that's my prime concern. You can call it my prime directive."

He figured it was okay to use those terms since she probably had never heard them used before and he also doubted that she'd ever experienced an android close to her, whether physically, sexually, or intellectually.

"So what you're saying is that you are an honorable man, and that you do not wish or desire to be repaid. Is that correct?"

"That would be correct. Totally accurate. I am not doing this to get paid or for some satisfaction for myself. I'm doing it because it's my duty, my job to protect you and people like you. That's all I do all day long. And I'm learning every day how to do that better and better."

"How long have you been doing this?"

This was an answer Adamis could give a specific time to. "About three and a half years now. So you see, I have much to learn. I really haven't had time to learn much about the female species."

"Something about the way you talk is different, unusual. Are you perhaps immune to women's affections? That's the only thing I can think of."

"Well, no, it's that I feel awkward. And it would be unfair of me to do this with you reeling under the abuse that you received. Let's focus on getting you well, okay?"

"If you're sure that's what you really want, I'm okay with that."

"Do you desire some food? I'm afraid I don't have much, as I've been on a fairly strict workout routine. But I don't suppose any of the things I have in my cupboards would be of interest to you. Tell me what you like to eat and I will prepare it for you or get it for you from somewhere else."

"And he cooks too. Where in the world have you been my whole life?" she asked him.

Adamis felt his cheeks go pink, which again was a new feeling. If he touched them, they'd be hot. He hoped that she didn't notice. He wasn't that lucky.

"Oh my God, you are blushing. You are inexperienced, aren't you?"

"I am experienced with some things, but when it has to do with affairs of the heart I'm afraid my experience has been limited to friendship."

"So no moonlight strolls holding someone's hand, no drinking champagne until you're drunk and ready to rip off all your clothes and go jump on somebody? That's never happened to you?"

"No. It hasn't. You might think I'm crazy, but all of my time I have been putting into my studies, and, if I wanted to be a man of the world, I would have signed up for something different."

He didn't need to tell her he had no choice in the matter, since he was created for the purpose he was now performing. But now that he'd been given his freedom, he had an ability to choose his path and, as long as he still stayed within the general guidelines, perhaps he could alter things slightly. But he knew one thing for sure, getting into an intimate relationship with this woman first of all was premature, but, secondly, probably not even close to being a good idea. It was one of the things that Darius had warned him about. Now the question was how to explain it to her in a way so that she wasn't offended, or didn't feel unworthy of being cared for. He needed some kind of scientific explanation, a deadline, a calling of some kind that superseded everything else in his life. And because that latter explanation was really the truth that's what he went with.

"Let me explain to you that I work for a very demanding corporation, and we are trying to right many wrongs in the world. We're working on being able to anticipate crime, evil, or wrongdoers. My job is to seek out and destroy ill-doers, people who interfere with certain things, namely authority, law and order, people who generally like to disrupt and control, manipulate or abuse people. I knew right away that the gentleman you were with was one of the people I was going to come up against over and over again. And I knew that you were the innocent party. And I don't care what your history is–or your past–it's just that in this particular situation I could clearly see that he was the perpetrator and you were the victim."

"Okay, I can buy that."

"When you are selected to do this particular work, it makes it all important what your whole life is like, not just the times when you are working, but when you are off as well. That's why I've always focused on just doing my job and, when I was not doing my job, I just focused on preparing myself to do my job the next day. There really has been little time for involvements, and I like to stay in good physical shape, I don't do dangerous things, and I want to be fully capable of performing my job at the highest level."

She nodded with apparent agreement.

"It doesn't require that I have a personal relationship with the people I am saving. It only requires that I'm healthy, that my body is able to counter any attack that may come against me or the person I'm trying to protect, and, other than that, my life is fairly complete and whole. And I'm happy. Is that so hard to see?" He had to force himself to add a smile after he said this last sentence. He could see she wasn't really accepting this last part but was going to leave it be for now.

"You said something about dinner or lunch? How about you taking me out to a restaurant?" she suddenly asked.

"Don't think it's wise. Your controller may be out looking for you as we speak. He might have had a change of heart. These types exact revenge—you know this. Besides, I don't think you're ready for that. I want to make sure you are not requiring something I cannot give you."

She pouted like a child. "You are absolutely no fun at all. Has anyone ever told you that?"

"Never." He saw her struggle. The wincing of her eyes was the telltale sign.

"I would prefer to go to the store and put together something that you like. You tell me. What are your favorites? I want you to stay here where you're safe. Once people see you and see you with me or without me, see you in this neighborhood, your presence will be noted, and somehow that information will get to the people you are trying to extricate yourself from. I hope you understand. This district is heavily monitored and has a strong police presence because of all the crime."

"Italian, then. I like Italian."

"Excuse me?"

"You said choose. I want Italian."

"Italian it is. It's also my favorite. I have a little bit of leftover from my dinner last night, if you'd like, I can heat it up. I go there once a week at minimum and I only eat half, and bring the other half home."

"I was hoping for the whole experience. You know. The music, the candles, the aromas from the kitchen."

Adamis could see that she was going to be a handful, questioning absolutely everything he was asking of her to do, but, in order to keep her safe, he had to do it.

"One thing concerns me. I need you to follow instructions. I need you to have respect for what I'm asking you to do in order to keep you safe. Is that too unreasonable?"

She shrugged. "No, I don't think it is. Am I allowed

to make requests?"

"Not just yet, please. Why don't we start by heating up the Italian food I brought home last night, and why don't you tell me about you, and your life. I'll start with your name. What is your name?"

"You first."

He was frustrated but had not lost his patience. "My name is Adamis. I was born and raised here in California. I work for a company across the bay, and I will be leaving that job shortly and making a move, perhaps across country. I have many things I need to do before I move, but one of the most important things I have to do is to see to it that you are well enough to be sent on your own. And that's my full focus. Right now, that's all I can share. There will be time for other things later."

"Well, my name is Emmy, and I also was raised in California. My parents were in and out of jail at different times and during one of those stretches, when both of them were behind bars, I had an uncle who sold me to a housekeeping service. I mean, he didn't say he sold me, he just told me that the house my parents had–I thought–owned, was going away, and I needed to find another place. This new housekeeping job would give me that kind of an arrangement, which would work. I didn't mind the work, and I didn't mind not being around my fighting parents all the time, or some of their friends, so I went to work for this concern."

"How sad. But I understand your circumstances. It adds a lot."

"After I was there for several months, I began to understand that the housekeeping service really wasn't that. I was expected to perform certain things for clients, especially wealthy clients, and my international passport was removed, my identification numbers were expunged, somehow eliminating me from the federal database, and I became a new person in a new place with a new job where nobody else knew who I was, and my uncle didn't know where I was. And I've lived that way for the last five years."

She hesitated for a few seconds, tapping the flesh under her eyes and removing tears starting to form there. "I've been close to death several times, I've been to the hospital on several occasions and had arms and legs casted for broken bones, both by my handlers and by those who had purchased time with me. I was to not tell on any of the people who did this, and I witnessed personally several who were eliminated because of their loose lips, so to speak. I'm a good person at heart, and I try to help other people when I can. To cope, I'm embarrassed to say I also have been using alcohol and drugs occasionally, and I must admit my decision-making is horrible. And the longer it went on, the more I thought to myself, maybe sometime, mercifully, I'd take an overdose and it would all be over. I never really looked forward to a future before. I've been wanting to die for at least the past two years. Does that surprise you?"

Her honest, brown eyes cut him to the core. He was shredded, left vulnerable, and felt her pain at the loss of her history, her life—a life filled with violence and pain. Adamis was stirred by her brief story. He needed to know more, just in case he felt the urge to get even with every single person who was responsible for putting this woman in such deep despair. For tempting her with Dr. Death, that cunning and evil bastard who lurked in the shadows and was skilled at ruining the world.

They would all underestimate him and his desire to never give up until every evildoer was irradiated from the globe, from the whole universe.

# CHAPTER 5

ADAMIS KNEW HE had to build the pretense that he required sleep, even though it was recommended–during his "sleep" time-that he instead listen to learning tapes or program himself for a plug-in to update information on certain digital speeds for his various components. Though it usually took only an hour or two, since Emmy would be watching his every move, it wouldn't be wise for him to stay up all night reading Darius' notes, even though he greatly wanted to.

He was still reeling from the stories that she told him. That's when he offered to allow her to sleep in the bed and he would take the couch. In that manner, if he felt like getting up and reading, he could do that in privacy. And, she could have her own privacy and a much more comfortable bed to recover in.

He was going to insist on this.

"It just doesn't seem fair for me to take the bed;

you've already been more than generous with your agreement to take care of me for a few days, but I don't want to push you out of your bed. And, since I can't tempt you to share your bed with me, I am grateful for your help, and for the kindness you've extended to me already. I just don't want to take more."

"As a matter of fact, Emmy, it would be easier for me to ensure your security by being on the outside of the bedroom door rather than on the inside of it. I can watch the windows and the doorways, which are the only two areas anyone could use to gain access to this condo. And sometimes I have difficulty sleeping, so I get up and read. This would make it so that I didn't disturb you. Trust me, I've slept many nights on this couch, fallen asleep watching the digital Dumbo."

She frowned at that. "Digital Dumbo?"

"Well, that's what I call it. It kind of looks like a great big elephant head, if you ask me. We have our screen in the middle and then the two large boom boxes on each side that look like an elephant's ears to me. I just look at that huge TV and I think of a huge animal."

She giggled at that. "I just don't know where you get all these sayings. It's just so odd to hear you speak this way. You're like a very worldly man, and yet you have these huge blind spots, and you seem to regress back maybe thirty or fifty years in your language. Our language is so fluid these days, especially with the voice enhancements people have made. You can trick anybody over the phone. That's why they've outlawed voice-activation devices on most security systems, or so I've been told."

He was impressed that perhaps she knew more than she had been letting on.

"That's true, and there are few safeguards against it. Usually a safe message or phrase is all that's required to stop that right in its tracks. But I understand. Please, accept my invitation to sleep on the most luxurious and comfortable bed you'll ever find in this whole universe."

"Well, then. How can I refuse?"

Adamis hunkered down on the leather couch, not bothering to place a sheet beneath him, smelling the leather and the tanning process that was still used, just like it was in the 21st century. *Some things never change,* he thought.

But he also detected her faint scent, probably not perceptible to humans, but for him it sent a sizzle down his spine and made his heart beat faster. He made a note of it to add to his research.

Over breakfast, he let Emmy know that he intended to visit several of his friends, since he was going to be looking for housing elsewhere. He also indicated he'd stop by for some groceries and asked her to make a list.

"So would it be possible for me to live here then—after you leave?" she asked him.

"I'm going to have to sell it. But if the new owner wants to rent it, I can make sure I put in a good word for you. I think you'd be better off staying further away from your handler."

"That's a good point. And then there's also the possibility that if I were to be able to afford a place someday, you could build me a shower just like yours."

"I'll tell you what, that's a promise. If you get together the money to purchase something, I would be happy to install you a shower. And, on second thought, it won't cost you anything."

Her eyes got big as saucers, and, despite her attempts to cover it up, she smiled widely, allowing some of her attractive exuberance to overflow. She was wearing the same pants as she had the day before, but a new shirt, one of Adamis' button-down long-sleeve shirts with the cuffs rolled to her elbows. Her skinny forearms hung like twigs from the oversized shirt.

He wondered if her scent would ever leave that shirt, or if he would ever want to wash it, and he didn't mind lending her these clothes, purely for his own self-interest. He might use it to meditate, and smiled at the thought.

Adamis reported to the laboratory at the Adam Group building, not the offices where he and Darius used to talk. These were the locations where research was being done by human and android scientists, where androids were de-parted, others were submitted for tuneups, and where several of his AI friends hung out. There was lots of gossip amongst the nonhuman, things they knew about their human handlers—who was screwing who, who had fondled their android, who was cheating on their wife, the sort of things humans didn't think about. Between his friends, there was a high level of trust, a sort of brotherhood.

Since any android could tell if another android was nearby, the group had certain code words they used, and nicknames for each other as well as their human handlers. The de-parter known as Ben was handy with a drill, which sounded like a bumble bee, so his nickname was "Bumble Bee," since it started with the same letter as Ben. One of the human wives–Sally–of Dr. Kemp (and he had three wives, which he thought was a secret), the androids heard clear across the lab when she and her husband were having sex in the android bathroom. She became "Screamer," and so it went.

It was, therefore, difficult to have any real secrets between his friends, or between androids and humans, since the "made" men and women could pick up minor changes in speech patterns, body sweat and other fluid levels, as well as circuitry anomalies. If something really had to be a secret, Adamis learned to shut off certain sensors and block detection, a feature Darius had built into him to avoid discovery of their research, done recently at a minor surgery last fall.

Not all, but Adamis and two or three others, were gifted with a form of telepathy, that allowed them to listen to thoughts. It worked well on their android friends, but Adamis had not had much luck with human thoughts. He cloaked the device more than he used it since he wasn't sure who actually had been given that capability.

"Look at you, looking all spiffy. You going out to party tonight?" Connor asked him. Connor had been a regenerated sex slave, well-endowed and legendary amongst the android set. He was a specialist in tuning up flailing libidos and even performing minor surgeries to adjust body parts that were elected to be enhanced. He'd even operated on a couple of the human researchers, a secret he'd told Adamis about, but which he kept very close to the vest.

Most of the time his work involved sexual organs. He was a good man, although it was difficult to tell when he was telling the truth. He had a nervous way of flicking his tongue over his upper teeth, making a little cricket-type sound that just annoyed Adamis no end. But it also was a warning sign which caused those around him to pay attention to who might be entering their space or who had turned on their mental scanners. Amongst friends, there was no good reason for this, but, amongst humans, the android group never fully trusted them. It was a power issue. Androids were known to be de-parted for saying the wrong thing to a human scientist or researcher, so they never expressed more than they needed to, and tried to keep all communications with humans vanilla.

Connor's group was in the middle of taking apart Emil, who was a library android, experienced in data management, but who was created and owned by an elderly woman who had passed away the week before. Nobody grieved over the death of these machines, even though it was well known that the android-human relationship was extremely symbiotic, similar to the relationship humans had with their pets, particularly dogs. But, in many ways, humans treated their dogs better. Androids never thought of themselves as pets, but the desire to be close to their maker, to learn from their maker, to please their maker, was overriding, probably because they'd been programmed with it.

Even then, most androids didn't trust them.

Adamis was different in that respect. Nothing

S. HAMIL

could shake his love for Darius, or his loyalty, which would be so until his eventual death.

"I'm sorry to see Emil go. He worked very hard. I think the library system will miss him. He probably did the work of ten or fifteen humans," Adamis said, reaching out to touch one of Emil's severed arms. The android's fingers responded still to the touch.

"Would you look at that? First time I've seen it too," said Connor, pointing to the touch between the now de-parted and Adamis.

"He was special. I enjoyed talking to him about books on occasion."

"Books? You take the time to read books? Hey, you just download everything you need to know!" said Leon, a senior member of Connor's team.

"You mean what they want you to know. Ever wonder where the downloads come from? Who makes up those feeds we insert every night?" Adamis asked them.

"Are we going anti-system here, buddy?" Connor said, wiping the black oil from his hands onto his apron, then cleaning them with a spray and dirty rag.

"He'll be missed. He knew things differently, things I've never heard of before. Things only find in books, not tablets or streaming downloads," said Adamis. He knew he would have to clean up that later, and made a note to remind himself before he left the building.

"Well, I think the librarians will miss him because he worked all night long too. Anybody would get that kind of recognition if they worked 24 hours in a row," said Leon.

"That's probably right. I think that's it. Just in case you don't think so, I understand the rules. Was it difficult sending him on his way?" he asked Connor.

"Sending him on his way? You mean to heaven? You're saying androids go to heaven?" Connor was covered in black oil, which was Emil's lubricant and mixed well with his synthetic blood type.

The android's head was sitting on the chair next to the de-parter, and with his eyes open, Adamis could almost imagine that he was still listening, still alive and sentient.

"Ah, hell, Adamis. I turn it off. You know I do. Yes. I liked Emil. And it's a shame his maker was so old, but he's had six good years, and he knew this was coming."

"Of course. Probably stupid of me to ask."

"Oh, it happens all the time, you know. Especially with the new ones. They wonder about life and death and what it means for them. If there would be a chance to be set free. Like every good prostitute hopes to find Mr. Right and get married and have kids. You know the story. For us, it's rather simple, isn't it?"

Though Adamis thought the opposite, especially after his encounters with Emmy, he agreed with his friend. "Yes, it is, rather cut and dry."

"Except in this case, it's cut and get acid and guts all over my apron and my hands. I'll never get all this stuff off. I'm going to be stained for weeks. And every time I look down at my brown hands, I'm going to think of Emil. I guess, in his own way, he's forcing us not to forget him."

The whole room burst out laughing, only because there were no humans present.

"So, what are they going to do with his parts? Has anyone claimed them?" asked Leon.

"I think the public library in Manhattan has requested his database. Nobody could catalog books as fast as he did, and he could just walk down the aisles and find every single book that was out of order just as fast as he could walk. It's amazing how well he kept that place in order. I think they're looking for someone with similar training, but it wasn't fashionable to create library androids; people seem to like the sexy ones instead. And some think books and preserving old books is a waste of time," said Adamis.

"Here, here. I think they're right," said Connor. "Don't go getting me in trouble with your thoughts of stealing books while they look for the replacement, Adamis."

And that gave him an idea. What if he could pick up a few of those precious books, even novels of the 21st century, before AI became the way of the world, a real book to own, for his journeys. Who would notice it now that Emil was off duty? He would think about this later, and made another note.

Instead, he changed the subject. "Have you ever thought about taking on a partner or having your maker create one for you?" Adamis asked his friend.

"Oh, that would be nuts. It would make life so much more complicated. Having to worry about someone else? Or, worse still, have someone nag you because you didn't worry about them when you switched off? Not for me. Besides, I think he'd just depart me just for thinking about it. It's ridiculous," answered Connor.

"They promise it sometimes, but I think it's the carrot and the stick type of thing. Just trying to keep the Indians happy while the cowboys get ready to launch a war. None of us gets out of this alive, but I have to say it's less painful for us than it is for most humans. There are some diseases and forms of death that are just horrible. I don't envy their humanness," added Leon. "Con, turning on the sanitizer now," he said as he reached over the operating table to pull a red lever.

"Roger that. Everyone back up and cover your pie holes," Connor barked.

The giant machine overhead roared to life, spewing out a bluish-green steam that covered the surface of Emil's parts, including his head. The room went up nearly ten degrees after the job was done. Connor turned on the exhaust while Leon turned back on the AC. Within minutes, the room was freshly scented, clean, and cool.

Adamis spoke next. "You make a good point there. I never thought of it that way. We do have the best of both worlds, don't we?"

Connor threw down his dirty apron into a laundry chute. "Absolutely. If I didn't believe that, I would run away and you would never find me again."

"I've no reason or desire to run away." He knew he had to lie about this. "I just hope Darius lives forever and then I get to spend all of my time learning everything he knows. He is such a genius at things. He knows everything."

"Does he know you love books?" asked Leon.

"He does. But he knows I don't have access to them." Adamis was lying and hoping he was getting away with it. Darius had let him hold a first edition copy of *Gulliver's Travels*, a book eventually given to him in the briefcase Darius left him. It was his most precious possession.

"Well, let's pray for his good health then," Connor said, handing Adamis an opened can of beer.

"I generally don't like beer in the morning. Do you?"

"I think it's good for my insomnia. By three o'clock in the afternoon, I'm ready for a nap. If I'm lucky, I sleep right through dinner. But I'm up by 7:00 or 8:00, to pee, from all the beer and the water I've had during the day, and then I'm ready to go back to sleep and only then can I sleep all night."

Just then Goshen, another one of Adamis' friends, entered the room. He was carrying a deceased female android who was missing her lower torso.

"Hey there, everyone. Good to see you, Adamis."

Adamis was surprised at how gingerly he laid the partially torn-apart android on the table.

"You want to help me do this one?" he asked Adamis.

"No, I just thought I'd stop by, and it had been a while so I thought I'd see how you guys were doing. You've got some great talent here who know far more than I."

"We'll help," Connor said gruffly. "Where the hell

is her lower half?"

"Beats me," said Goshen. "I guess her maker kept it. Kinda odd, if you ask me."

"Jeez, it must have been his favorite body part. Who was her maker? He still alive?" asked Connor.

"Yup. He wants us to make another model, but a 'fizzy model,' as he said. I'm going to have to ask one of the scientists what that means," Goshen replied.

"It's a human-like android vibrator and vacuum device. Sort of a kinky request, don't you think?" Connor added.

"Yeah. Figures. Her maker was Director Hamstead. You know, Department of Android Security?"

No one said anything further. Adamis saw Connor inspecting the partial AI, looking for recording devices.

"You suspect a trap?" asked Adamis.

"What do you think? I don't see anything, though."

Goshen scanned the table with Emil's body parts spread out, sparkling clean. "I didn't know about Emil, and I'm sorry. I will miss him."

"I don't want to be missed. I just want to be forgotten." Connor said. Leon laughed.

Adamis found it odd. "Don't you like living? Don't you like the life that we've been given?"

Both men looked up from their work, and said in unison, "What life?"

"You mean whose life, right?" Adamis asked them.

"We are made up of other people. The original Frankenstein, if you will. I loved that movie, I just did. I watch it at least a couple times a year. It was so sad in the end, but he decided it was worth it since he had found his true love."

"I'll have to listen to that one again. It's hard for me to watch some movies," said Adamis. "I feel like I should be doing something, not just sitting there, being entertained."

"Watch it, you could be accused of describing human teenagers. They do it all the time, and it doesn't bother them at all."

"But they have the gift of life, don't they?" Adamis said.

"That's true enough. Maybe if their life was programmed to be shorter, like ours is, they would learn the sweetness of living for only a few years. We don't know before we were parted and put together, we don't know whose parts we have and whose parts we don't, and we know how to turn off any anxiousness or feelings of anxiety as we accept new parts into our body. We have a long ways to go before we become perfect, don't we, Adamis?"

Adamis smiled. Darius had lovingly called him the most perfect being he'd ever created. He was going to remember that meeting, that clip, for as long as he was able.

"Well, I'm going to let you farts work on your projects here. When are they picking up the pieces?" Adamis asked.

"You haven't heard the edict?" asked Connor.

Adamis figured he'd been so focused on his new life and the potential it held for him that he'd missed some important news flash. "What news?"

"They've decided that they're going to form a clearing house for all parts. It's going to be calculated as a national treasure. Can you believe that? They don't find that we are a national treasure, but once we are departed and segregated into bins, legs and arms together, eyes and heads, and guts and toenails, and everything that we're made up of, once we're parted those pieces are worth more than the sum of the parts in a working, active android. What kind of human being made up that rule? Can you answer me that? Adamis?"

Adamis was thinking that it probably was an evildoer.

"Someone who didn't want the parts used by other androids to fix themselves. It sort of takes control from us, doesn't it?" he answered.

"Holy shit, you're right! How did you get to be so

smart?" asked Leon.

*Because I am loved,* Adamis thought to himself.

That gave him another thought, and he quickly masked it. Maybe he should visit the creator of this edict, and maybe it would do the world some good to have him disappear. He'd do it sometime when he's able. Maybe he should also look into the Director's lifestyle. Surely there was abuse going on in his household if these were his special requests.

But, right now, he had bigger problems. He had a beautiful woman sleeping in his bed, and, forever after–when she left–he would never sleep in that bed the same way again. He had no use for thinking about edicts or some cretin's weird sexual appetites. He had no respect for rules, either.

Because Adamis was about to break them all.

# CHAPTER 6

T HERE WERE PROBABLY half a dozen items that Adamis knew he had to purchase, but at the top of his list was a communication device, preferably an easy to use cell phone, so that he and Emmy could communicate whenever he wasn't home. It also might solve the worry he had about her leaving the condo and going out to pick up items she needed. And he already knew she was curious. If they had a means to communicate, she could request that he get it for her on his way home.

He knew of a district in the Emery Victory project area, formerly known for its slums and poor conditions but now rehabilitated into shining crystal housing–still for homeless and disadvantaged but without the normal issues of street crime. The area was heavily controlled, heavily policed, but it also was subject to much corruption. And, depending on who was appointed, it was a very rich and lucrative job to be the

Superintendent of Security for this area. He had befriended the current superintendent at first, when he was undersecretary, until Mr. Orefos was murdered in some kind of a drug deal gone bad. After that, the new superintendent unfriended him. He knew that public officials had to be careful about making friendships with androids, so it didn't bother him.

But he had learned quite a bit about the community, and he knew there was a district no one else–or not many others–knew about, where they specialized in black market electronic devices, repeaters, scanners, relays, forward switches and cell phones. He knew of a dealer who specialized in old model cell phones, things he procured from the estates of people who had passed on. They had old technology, which is to say they weren't as traceable, and even an untraceable brand new phone was traceable. This required access to old technology, and a used older phone was something he was looking for.

Cortez Cisco was the gentleman he was looking for. Adamis found him sitting at a table in the back of a restaurant his family owned. Cortez greeted him warmly. He was human, but treated androids and humans, if they could be trusted, equally. Adamis couldn't afford to feel the same way.

"Hola, amigo! Are you hungry? My mother has just

made some fresh tamales."

"No, but I'll take some home if you don't mind. How about I purchase a half dozen, if you have that many to spare?"

"Don't be silly, Adamis. I won't take your credits. You have to learn to be taken care of."

Adamis reacted to that, nearly showing anger. "I am well taken care of, Cortez, and I intend to keep it that way too."

He pulled out a chit from his wallet, which would pay for the tamales and give his mother a generous tip. "For your mother, then."

"For my mother," Cortez said as he slipped the paper note into his pocket. He held up six fingers to the older woman behind the bar and she retreated to the kitchen to prepare the to-go order.

"So maybe you'll take all that back when you hear my request." Adamis noted that Cisco seemed to be in good spirits, he was crisply dressed, sported an expensive sculpted beard that was shaved into ridges and wings at the side, a design almost looking like a face tattoo. His hair also was buzzed quite short, with zigzag lines like some would see dread lines, except it made him look like his head was full of lightning. And his hair was bleached, and then dyed electric turquoise.

It was pretty in your face, not something Adamis

would like, but he understood it was his calling card. It showed that he was successful, and he was not a bureaucrat. That was probably the most important thing to let people know about.

"So what is it you're looking for? I can't imagine that Darius would leave you wanting for anything."

"Well, I have met someone, and I wish to communicate with her if I could."

"Behind his back?" Cortez asked. He leaned forward, his upper torso on his elbows as he leaned into them across the table. He was grinning from ear to ear and most anxious to hear the story. "Do tell me. You won't get anything unless you tell me."

"I have come to the decision that I should seek a companion, perhaps a girlfriend. We are not sure it would be the type of relationship that Darius would understand, but I do intend to tell him. I just hope he doesn't get angry with me."

Cortez leaned back in his chair with a squeak, crossed his legs, and nodded his head very slowly, studying Adamis. "I can't believe that I'm hearing this. From you?"

"Look, I have done you some favors in the past, nothing illegal, and–"

"For which I am eternally grateful, and, yes, my nephew is doing fine, and has remained out of jail."

"That's truly good to hear, especially since he never belonged there anyway. He was a victim of a more powerful warlord. I am so sorry that he was subjected to his brutality. I hope he has learned his lesson."

Cortez shrugged. "Well, as I told my sister, he will either learn or he will die at a very young age. You know we are losing a lot of our young people these days. So much corruption out there."

Adamis had forgotten about the seedy underside of society. He had been concentrating so much on all the exciting things that Darius had been teaching him, learning so much and gaining in knowledge and strength, his moral fiber becoming stronger every single day, that he'd forgotten that the rest of the world perhaps was not moving along at the same pace. It even appeared to be going in the opposite direction.

"Well, I hope he has learned his lesson. What I'm here for, Cortez, is a cell phone, or a pair of cell phones. Darius has told me that it's time for my training of a different nature, if you know what I mean."

"Sex. He wants to teach you about sex. What does Darius want with a cell phone? Are we talking about phone sex, then?"

"No, not that. I want to obtain a way to talk or message her when we aren't together. And I'm feeling funny about it. I thought that perhaps I could experiment on my own. Now I understand some of these things have to be granted permission for and he said he was writing a grant or a proposal to get me a companion so I could understand the concepts. He thought it would further my development."

"And it would. It truly would. It will mess with your head as well as your balls and every other cell in your body. You think a woman is worth it? Honestly? And have you found a suitable android woman? Why don't you just turn on her telepathy? Surely you could have Darius adjust her control center."

"I just don't want to let him know at the current time and I would like to explore a bit by myself." Adamis thought about the next line he was going to speak and almost didn't say it. But at last he decided to just give it a try. "I think that doing something secret and behind Darius' back might make it more exciting for me. For the way I was built and developed, it is not difficult for me to get excited about scientific studies and reading journals and learning about theories and mathematics, quantum physics, the molecular biology of humans and androids. All those things are exciting and fascinating to me. But I often feel awkward around others. Other androids and humans. And most of my friends, not all, but most, are men. I thought I would try to form a relationship. And I found someone who is compatible."

"Have you ever had sex, Adamis?"

"No. And you can't ever tell anyone this, please. As a matter of fact, we may not even have sex. It could be a ways off. But I like to be prepared."

"If I wasn't confident I could keep my mouth shut, I wouldn't ask so many questions. Let me tell you something though. You should never tell anyone else about this. You are too trusting. I will help you, but be very, very careful."

Adamis did appreciate his friendship, and his discretion, and that was when he was certain he could put his trust in this man.

"So, I want an old model cell phone that cannot be traced. I want it set up so that only she and I can communicate with each other, that it won't pick up or seek any other devices nearby, that it won't give off a signal to anyone or anything other than this other cell phone that I will have. I do not want these phones to have access to the internet; it is purely a communication device, very cut and dry. Nothing fancy, but–"

"Nothing anyone could ever trace. I understand, and I have such phones for you."

Adamis was relieved.

"You come back here in three days at around four

o'clock in the afternoon, and I will have them for you. Can I meet this woman?"

"No. She has to remain unknown. I can't jeopardize her safety. It would only be in an emergency."

"Very well. I'll see you in three days then. And, Adamis, remember what I told you? Don't trust anyone, especially a human."

"That's why I'm not going to bring her with me."

On the way home, Adamis smelled the package of foil-wrapped tamales, and was immediately struck by pangs of hunger. He thought Emmy would enjoy the feast.

It was going to rain again, but didn't look imminent, so he thought he'd try one more stop before he went home. He knew tonight he was going to have a long message for Darius, since so much had happened in the last day, and he wasn't sure how much more walking around he wanted to do. The ruse of the freedom–and Darius' upcoming death–was weighing heavy on him.

He decided to go visit the Security Chicks–the name all the other AI androids chose for them. They were the AI tactical girls who helped the police force do stings and special operations, often sent in to burning buildings to rescue humans or, with their superior jumping and climbing skills, scale a 30-story building without using a ladder or waiting for a fire truck. They were often temporarily murdered, and then brought back to life, their lab being adept at making their shutdown as small and the least invasive as possible, so that all their memories were intact. And they were also known to be ill-treated by the police officers they served. In fact, he'd been told that the guard dogs and police dogs, especially the drug-sniffing dogs, were treated much better.

But this allowed the local police to sit back and send someone else in to do the dangerous and dirty things while they got to claim the credit, stay out of trouble in case it went sideways, as well as capture the badges and metals. The number of apprehensions made always added to their monthly pay, so the Security Chicks were busy almost night and day, since they didn't require sleep.

The Security Chicks lived on a houseboat anchored in the San Francisco Bay. It was a huge vessel, commandeered in a cruise ship pirate raid, not one of the ships that held thousands of passengers, but an exclusive 100-cabin private vessel that catered to the rich and famous back in the day. Somehow the police had confiscated it, and they were allowed to use it as a dormitory, first for new recruits and trainees, and then for the Chicks.

This was an all AI woman task force. It was dangerous for them to live in the general population, Adamis had been told, so their sisterhood was a very tight-knit group, difficult to penetrate, but a force all its own. Still, Adamis had been told that they frequently were abused by their especially male policemen handlers.

There was a long pier that came out from the shoreline where the ship was docked. The large engines were working 24/7, keeping the air conditioning running, since everything was run by the nuclear reactor on board. It was not a drain on society to have this luxury vessel used as housing, and all of the women were tough as nails, but they were androids, so they couldn't remain overheated for days on end. This was the most efficient way–and cheapest cost–to have them at the ready anytime of the day or night.

Their AI abilities were off the charts, aided with special detectors and devices implanted in their taste, smell, and eyesight. They had better skills in that direction than even Adamis did.

A group of five of the Chicks waited for him and had started to gather before he was more than two or three steps on the pier. All five of them were fully armed with weapons strapped to their torsos. They never adopted anything but a police uniform and

Adamis had never seen any of them in a dress. It was common they would all have the same tattoos, they bought the same sunglasses, they were issued the same combat boots, and even their waterproof uniforms were identical. It was a badge of honor to be placed in one of these units. This particular one, originally the first of its kind, housed roughly 50 to 60 AI ladies.

"Hey there to the ship, and the Chicks that live on it!" said Adamis.

"Hey there yourself, and state your purpose even though you're friend," One of the women shouted back at him.

He waited until he was within a few feet, not wanting the whole Bay to hear him. It often created a bowl-like atmosphere. It was said prisoners at Alcatraz, back in the day, could lean into their tiny windows and hear people dancing and partying at Fishermen's Wharf miles away. The warden had installed those windows just for that purpose so they could contemplate what they were losing by following their life of crime.

In normal voice, he continued, "Cherry, my reasons are purely social. I just wanted to check with you guys because we hadn't had communications for some time. Is there anything you want me to look into or research as far as wayward androids or trends in human development?" he asked as he met them at their gate. They had installed some sort of crest on the front, a Coat of Arms like plaque.

Cherry was a huge android woman, and Adamis thought that perhaps her beginnings started as a man, but then someone changed their mind and made her female. But her muscles were easily twice those of anyone else's, and, like all of them, she wore her hair short. She was often used in quelling riots and gang-land shootings, because she was so formidable in her size and speed. Her hands were specially fitted with metal plates and her reaction times were such that she could fend off most rounds, even semi-automatic. It would take a small bomb to incapacitate her. And, even on those two occasions when someone used one, she was fully restored and put back into service within a month. She was a remarkable woman, and Adamis loved studying her.

"Permission granted. You better behave though; we don't let just ordinary people on board, you know that."

"I've got no agenda, no messages, and nothing I'm looking to buy, sell, or get. I'm just here to say hello and double-check make sure everything's okay with you guys, and see if there's anything I can be of service. I like it when you tell me somebody's doing something wrong, and I can go pick them up for you or take care of the individual myself. You got any comers?" Adamis asked.

"You get your butt inside here, and we'll talk." Cherry said. She scanned the shore before she closed the gate behind them all.

Two other women Adamis didn't recognize followed them inside the grand lobby, which functioned as their living room, although it was nearly the size of a ballroom in a hotel. They had parties, dances, and feasts, but, to get an invitation to this ship, you had to be somebody very special, and rarely did it include the handlers who took care of them.

"I've got two new titanium arms, Adamis." She held her well-oiled and muscled arms in the air like a champion. "Just got them put in a month ago."

"Impressive. What happened to the others? They looked pretty useful on the surface."

"I've been begging. I practically have had to suck that fucker's dick to get my arms; the ones I got were no good. I don't know who's making these things these days, but it was just terrible. Painful, too slow; I got hit with a round just because I couldn't get my hands up in time. That was when I just had it."

The other two women laughed at her. Nodding, agreeing with her story.

"She pulled the round out with her fingers and

pressed it into that asshole's forehead."

All of them chuckled, sounding like a coven of witches.

Adamis liked Cherry's spirit and he could see how formidable she could be, even to her handler. Her handler was a local beat cop, not an important or impressive person, and he was good at negotiation for hostages. But, if that failed, he would send Cherry in, in a heartbeat. It was the carrot or the stick, and most people, if they were asked, would rather deal with the carrot than Cherry, the stick. As a policeman, her handler was more sensitive than many of the rest of them.

One of the other ladies asked Adamis if he wanted a drink.

"Just some water, please, if you have it and some ice maybe?"

"You got it," she said.

"So Lisa here has something you might be interested in. We've got some new guys on the force in San Francisco, and they're a real strange bunch. A little bit on the blue side, if you know what I mean," Cherry said.

"You mean they're abusive, or they get off on being abusive?" he asked.

"Mm-hmm," she nodded.

"How many? And what department?"

"The ones Lisa's met are I think six, right, Lis?" She turned and addressed a diminutive AI with huge brown eyes.

"There are six of them there now but they're bringing in a whole department. We've been told that they are not bringing their own AIs with them, that we will be loaned out to them. I spent an afternoon with one of them, and, when we were done, he pretty much—well, he raped me, Adamis. I never had that done before. I could have fought him off, but I was afraid to. Know what I mean?"

"Just for the record, she's had sex before this, but not with a human. And that's against the law, isn't it?" Cherry asked him.

"If you get me their names I can do some inquiries. But I have to be careful. Your guys won't help you out?"

"Fuck, no. I thought maybe the female cops on the force would help us, and two of us went to go speak with them, and they didn't want to touch it. There's something real black and bad going on over there at the office. I don't know why they would all of a sudden have to bring in such a goon force. But it's almost like they're expecting some kind of a big revolution or street riots, like they had years ago, if you remember.

They're gearing up for something, Adamis. I just don't know what it is, and nobody's letting on."

Lisa added, "Well, you know how it goes, Adamis, we don't need to know because we're expendable. I mean it's not going to change ever, but, for the sake of the public that we're supposed to be protecting, I mean somebody should look into it."

Cherry broke in. "They've definitely got something planned and I sure hope it's not some kind of a revolution that some guy in the federal system has got cooked up. San Francisco's getting to be a very dangerous place. And we're also being told that there's going to be a prison ship docked right next to us, and part of our responsibilities are going to be to make sure those guys never escape. I mean, that means we're going to be prison wardens, not in the field. Now does that sound like to you we're being decommissioned or we're getting to do something new because it's better?" asked Cherry.

"I think you're right. Something's wrong. With everything we've got going, it might take me a day or two. And Darius has a few little medical things going on so he's gone in for testing, but I'll bring it up just as soon as I talk to him next, but soon. It's probably something he'd want me to look into but let me ask him first."

"You know, Adamis, I like you. I think you're the

best of all of us, but I don't understand for the life of me why you trust any human being. I just don't get it," said Cherry.

"Because I truly believe he cares for me. I truly believe he will do whatever's good for me, whatever's right. He's not an android, he doesn't have AI, he's human, but he's one of those humans worthy of our trust. If he says I should go after them, then, Cherry, I will. But you can't tell anybody I'm doing that. I mean I've got to trust you. Nothing more needs to be said about it. But you might find a few guys floating in the bay."

"You know, Adamis, nothing would please me more. You'd have my undying loyalty. Thanks."

# CHAPTER 7

A DAMIS STOPPED AT his neighborhood store, picked up some eggs and milk, half and half, some cheese, and a few other things that he thought Emmy would like. He also bought some bread for toast and then just drew a blank. It would be so much easier, he thought, when he could communicate more, or when he could strategize more what to get and when to get it.

His days were going to be more intense, especially with the new wrinkle of Emmy and her needs, his responsibility to get her safely on her way. She was healing so fast, he almost thought she had some android DNA, or perhaps her closeness to him had caused her cells to awaken and heal faster. So he was running out of time, time to properly plan, ask his last questions, get an order going so he could leave the area long before anyone would be looking for him. And that meant getting her safely tucked some place where she would have no fear of being found.

As a result, every single hour was becoming more and more precious. He needed to also warn her that he was going to be distracted, that he'd need planning time. He had to do research now for the Chicks, but also he needed to find his forever home, the place he would move to permanently. And he really had no idea where to go. And he needed to find a place for Emmy.

The Pakistani clerk looked at him funny, a question resident there.

"Adamis, you don't usually buy eggs and cheese and bread. Are you changing your diet?"

"Just trying something new. You know, sometimes things get boring. I like to mix it up a bit."

"Yes, but this, this looks like you have company. These aren't your foods at all."

The old, wizened gentleman stared at him, and Adamis could see in his eyes that he knew the secret. He knew somehow. This human was wise beyond his human years, and maybe he'd experienced unusual things in his lifetime, but somehow he was exposed to happenings around the edges, registering that there was an ill wind afloat. It skirted the edges, keeping its secrets, causing him to be protective, careful, questioning. He knew something was happening. And it was going to be big.

"You have a family, Noral," Adamis asked.

"Yes, yes, I have family, but they do not live with me."

"Oh? Do they live in the United States?"

"It is not safe, Adamis. I am sending money home, but it will not always be this way." He stared into Adamis' eyes, almost as if trying to import meaning. Adamis upped his human telepathy and, sure enough, there was a message there from him. *You need to move on,* was his message. *This is not a safe place. People are watching.*

It hit Adamis like an electric shock. With so much coming up in the next few days or weeks or months, how was it that everybody seemed to have their own particular fear or slant on upcoming news. Adamis was going to be leaving, so why would they be telling him all this? Was he expected to somehow save them? He didn't quite understand why he was being made privy to all of this.

"Well, I hope your family is safe. You are a good man to care for them. I'm sure they appreciate you living in a dangerous place, just so they can have food to eat."

The man bagged up his items without saying a word, and handed him the package. "You as well. You take care. You–and your family."

Adamis turned and left the shop, suddenly feeling like he was never going to see this man again. It had been almost a daily occurrence that he would say hello to him, but today for some reason felt like the final farewell, just like he was saying farewell to some of his AI friends.

He'd promised, so he would help find somebody and make an effort to help the Chicks, but he wasn't sure he was going to be able to stay around long enough to really solve their problem. But maybe Darius could help put someone else in charge. That was just one more thing he would talk to him about tonight.

After he closed the door behind him, hearing the little familiar tinkle of the bell sounding in the background, he turned and looked back at the shopkeeper through the glass. The man waved to him. Now Adamis was sure this was the final time he would ever see this man.

He wondered what was going on in the world that was forcing all this change. Normally, his AI buddies kept to themselves, especially the AI crowd he hung with at the lab. They did their jobs, they gossiped a little bit, but they basically were happy just being of service. It didn't extend beyond that. But now, the whole community seemed to be worried about something looming on the horizon.

He rounded the corner to his condo, used his key card, let himself in through the doors and greeted the security agent at the front desk. Angela wasn't present today. It was a new guard, in a police uniform, which was a first as well. He greeted him and then went past him to the elevators.

"Excuse me, excuse me, but you have to sign in now. We have new rules."

"I'm sorry. I wasn't aware there were new rules."

"Yessir. Just started today."

"What happened to the other crowd? I'd gotten so used to seeing them. Is it a new company in charge now? Is that what's generating all of this?"

"Yes. There's new ownership of the downstairs, of the land beneath the building. You are an owner here?" he asked.

"Why would someone own the land underneath the building and the lower floor? You mean like the lobby area?"

"The bathrooms, the rec room, the meeting rooms, and, yes, the ground. All the other floors are owned by the co-op, which I assume means you as part of that."

"I didn't hear anything about that."

"Well, that isn't exactly something that would require your approval, so we are representing and protecting the interests of the new owners. The new owners require for anyone to pass through to show their card, their identification, and to sign in."

Unlike most people, in light of what was going to befall Adamis and Darius in their separation, one of the things he was the most concerned about was his leaving DNA traces behind. He was handed a pen, which he declined.

"I have my own pen, if you don't mind," Adamis said.

"Excuse me, sir, but you must use this one."

Adamis was irritated, but also alarmed with this turn of events. Aware that there were items that would record DNA and other information about the person who touched those items, and a pen or a pencil would be a perfect way to do that. You had to press on the sides, you would leave bodily fluids and oils and there would no doubt be skin cells left behind. He couldn't do that.

Again, he objected.

"Suit yourself, but you won't be able to enter the building or elevator, then."

So this was real. It was a real thing. That's all he could describe it as. A thing.

Finally, Adamis agreed. Picking up the pen with his fingers tucked into the bottom sleeve of his coat, so that none of his flesh touched the pen, he leaned over so that the guard couldn't see and signed his name without touching the side of his hand to the page. He dropped the pen on the marble countertop, and stated, "There you go. Now you must see my identification, is that correct?"

"Yes, sir."

As Adamis rummaged through his wallet, producing his security card, his international identification passport, and his ID card as being an employee of the Adam Group, the guard took a careful look.

"You are Adamis Jefferson?"

"Yes, sir, I am. You know the company?"

"We manage that building as well."

"But I thought Darius Jefferson owned it. He owns all of it."

"Well, he doesn't own the dirt."

"I believe he does. When did this happen?"

"It's a recent court decision. The county, to whom he pays taxes, assigned their interest in the property to a new corporation. Jefferson owns the building, including the walls and roof. He even owns the pipes that bring in water, electrical and gas. But he doesn't own the land. The recent court case determined that the taxing authority can sell their interest. And they did."

"Like I asked, when?"

"Oh, it's been in the works for some time. You'd have to research the records to find out. But, just like this building, we manage the owner's interest in the land. Think of it this way. He no longer has to hire security for protection. He has the corporation protecting him."

"What corporation?"

"Now I know you're joking, right?"

"No, I've not heard of this."

"The Corporation for Public Protection."

"I see. Well that certainly explains it. Thank you for this head's up." Adamis was even more worried than before. He attempted to scan the guard, but he wore a cloaking device, a new one Adamis hadn't cracked yet. He began to gather his things and head to the elevator.

"So you are the son of Darius Jefferson, I presume?" the guard said after him, just as the elevator doors opened.

Adamis didn't want to answer his question, so he evaded.

"Oh, you know him, then? He is a wonderful man even though we don't always see eye to eye." He smiled, and found that the guard was caught slightly off guard by his handsomeness.

"It's the same with my son. He's very bright, has big plans for the world, but he never listens to me. You, on the other hand, seem quite well put together. I'm pleased to know you." He held out his hand for a shake, and Adamis was forced to give him a firm handshake in return.

"I hope we see each other again," Adamis said as he withdrew his hand.

"I'll be here until midnight, then tomorrow will be somebody else. They'll all be new for a while. We have sixty new hires, and we manage several buildings all over the city. We even have properties in San Francisco, including City Hall."

"Impressive. Well, I wish you good evening, and I'll probably see you the next time you're on."

Adamis picked up his bags and skirted the edge of the counter, using the tip of the plastic bag to press his finger through to the elevator. Inside the elevator he used his card to get him to the 16th floor.

Once the doors closed, he almost dropped his packages and let out a sigh of relief, until he remembered that there were cameras in the elevator. When he got off at the 16th floor, he knew there were cameras every four doors, and probably some in his apartment that he was not aware of. He was going to have to be very careful with his conversation with Darius tonight, probably limited to just text messages back and forth. There would be no chance for a phone call, not with

Emmy being present and not with some of the restrictions and changes he was feeling. He'd never worried about his world before, but now everything seemed to be a problem.

At his door he slipped the card into the key slot, heard the click, and was inside. Once he opened the door, the room appeared to be filled with an oily smoke, seeming to come from the kitchen, and it obviously was something that Emmy was preparing. She'd opened the sliding glass door to the outside, something he'd asked her not to do. It not only wasn't safe, it kicked off the AC, making the whole place stifling hot.

"Is that you, Adamis?" she shouted from the kitchen, trying to make her voice carry over the sound of the fan.

"It's me. I didn't know you would find enough things to cook." He walked into the kitchen and saw her with the baggy jeans and shirt, a towel draped around her neck she was using as an apron. She had spattered grease all over the kitchen frying sausages.

"Where did you get those?"

"Your condo has free delivery service, and the food can be ordered and placed on your account."

"But how did you order it?"

"I talked to the gentleman downstairs, he was not

at the desk, but he was a janitor. I asked him how far to the supermarket, and he told me that there was a way we could order direct. He said you have the tablet in your room so I found it in your bedroom, and placed the order there."

"Which tablet?"

"The one on your nightstand. It controls the AC and the shades and everything else in this place, and it has a feature for home shopping."

"Did you have to give my name or your name?"

"I'm not stupid, Adamis. I used your name of course. It's not a voice request; it is digital, all digital. They didn't ask for any identification because the tablet is wired to this place, and I assume you will get the bill whenever you pay the mortgage or the fees for staying here. You have extra fees or charges that they levy on you each month with this ownership?"

"Yes."

Adamis was getting more and more nervous as the minutes of this day were drawing to a close. So much was becoming unstable, and he was uneasy and out of sorts for some reason. Emmy seemed to be in a wonderful mood.

"How are you feeling? Your wounds, your shoulder?"

She moved the pan off of the burner, and covered

it, then walked over to him, unbuttoning the top of the shirt she was wearing—his shirt. She showed him the bruise just at the base of her neck where her clavicle bone was located, and indicated to him that some of the purple bruising had begun to dissipate. Adamis could see this for himself. But he was also distracted with the look of the cleavage of her bra, the whiteness and smooth texture of her skin that he touched under the guise of examining her collarbone, and was attracted in so many ways to this woman he was almost afraid of all those emotions building up inside him.

"Do you like to touch me that way, Adamis?" Her large brown eyes peered straight into his soul. Her soft, supple lips hungry and whispering, pleading with him. Her voice was low and purring.

"I do. I am trying not to, but I do." His voice cracked.

"So are you hungry or are you hungry for me?"

"I, I." He couldn't speak because she had covered his mouth with her lips. Her tongue circled the inside of his mouth, forcing his lips open and darting in and out. He had no choice but to wrap his arms around her and press her hard against his body, one hand feeling the soft curvature of her back, the fingers gently slipping into the back of her pants where miraculously she wore nothing else beneath the denim.

She gasped. "Adamis, I want you to touch me all over."

He pulled his hand away, embarrassed.

"I will show you. Let me show you what it's like. I would like to be your first."

Adamis was wondering if he should cut this off and give his maker a call, an emergency call. He feared that if this was his first, if she was going to become his first, she might also become his last.

# CHAPTER 8

EMMY CAREFULLY MADE sure everything on the stove was turned off. She left the fan on, and took his hand. Like a child, he followed her into the bedroom, almost as an unwilling participant. His hesitation was gripping his belly; he was lost between two different lands, one the landscape of his freedom and what could be for the rest of his life, the other all the security and happiness he had known as a being created to be perfect. And was there any perfection in learning about sex without his maker's permission?

He was not a boy; he was made a man from the beginning, never having had a childhood. But he still felt like he should have to get permission for this. He tried to stop Emmy from disrobing him, but it was a futile gesture. She stood in front of him completely naked, standing over his white shirt, both of them standing over his pants. And then the pants he was wearing were on the floor, and next she removed his underwear and, before he could say a word, her hands cupped his balls and stroked him.

"Oh my." He said in spite of himself, sucking in air.

She came to her knees in front of him and looked up. "Adamis, look at me. Watch what I'm going to do. Look at me, encourage me, will you?"

"Emmy, I don't think I should–"

And then, as he did what she asked and watched her, she took him in her hands and inserted his member into her mouth, sucking hard, stroking him up and down his shaft with her tongue and lips.

It was such a delicious feeling. She pulled it out and licked both the pointed head and underside with her pink tongue, ran her canines down very gently, just enough to make a sharp impression, but not hurting him. She fondled his balls and then took his sack in her mouth and sucked them carefully, lovingly, until he was so rigid with his member that he felt like he was going to explode.

She stood, naked, incredible in the moonlight, her flesh calling out to his flesh, begging to be touched, teasing him from their frontsides. She allowed his thigh to press between her legs, rubbing against her sex, stroking her nether lips against his flesh, her moistness and her liquids traveling up and down as she pressed herself against him and tilted her head back, looking at him out of the slits of her eyes. Breathlessly. she whispered to him, "Isn't this much better? Don't you love this, Adamis?"

"I–I don't know what to say."

"Do you know what fucking is?"

Her head was at his chest, as she sucked on his nipples and kissed him, allowing her tongue to linger, and then sweeping up the side of his neck to find his lips again, where she gave herself to him and took from him all over again. When his mouth was free, he whispered, "Yes, I think I know."

Her face was inches away from his; he could still smell her lips and the scent of where her lips had been. He smelled her natural scent, and then the perfume she had put on, realizing it was his own aftershave she was wearing, his favorite scent, an old recipe belonging to the General George Washington himself, but it smelled completely different on her flesh.

"I want you to fuck me. I want you to try to fuck me hard. You can't hurt me. I'm going to show you. And then I want you to do it again."

She brought her hands up from fondling his balls to the sides of his face, gripping his ears and lacing her fingers through his hair.

She leaned into him and pressed her enormous breasts against him. "Can you do that, Adamis?"

"I don't know. But I want to. I don't know how it's done."

"You're nervous, aren't you?" she asked, smiling.

"Yes." His breathing was labored. She probably picked up all his fear and worry. "I want to do it right, but I'm still not certain this is something I should do. Should I have more training first?"

She twisted her head and looked at him sideways. "Are you for real? Why would you say something like that? You don't require any training. You're a man and I'm a woman. It's the most natural thing in the world. Why would you be afraid? I'm not going to hurt you."

"No, I believe you. I just don't know–"

"I have an idea. Let's go to your favorite room in the condo."

At first, he wasn't sure what room she meant, and then he saw the sparkle in her eyes and realized she was talking about his shower, the custom cubicle that she wanted him to build her someday.

"Okay, let's do that."

He followed her naked body into the bathroom, allowing her to turn on the water which automatically delivered at 95 degrees. She got out her washcloth he'd set aside for her, soaked it, and then started pressing it against her breasts, her upper arms, her neck, and turned around handing it to him so he could wash her back. He found the washing extremely pleasant, more pleasant than two days before when he found her, when he brought her back and washed her. Her skin was like silk, and, under the soapy suds, the washcloth and his fingers traveled, feeling how her skin was aroused by his touch.

He set the washcloth on the shower ledge and smoothed the suds all over her shoulders and back, with his hands–his palms first, and then his fingers. She handed him the soap again and he used it to bring more bubbles and soap to her body, making sure that her arms were clean, her forearms, her fingers. His strong fingers even dove up into her lower scalp and massaged, sending her into leaning toward him with a moan he loved hearing. He felt his member still enlarged, and getting larger by the minute. He couldn't–he tried to–but he couldn't avoid smashing against her backside. And each time his member touched her, she moaned again and reached for him, lovingly stroking him, lovingly showing her need for him.

She turned around and pressed the soap to his chest, looking up into his eyes, his face.

"I think you are the nicest, most handsome man I have ever met in my entire life. When I woke up and when I saw that you had rescued me . . ." She allowed her hands to trim the back of his neck. She whispered, "I thought I had gone, died, and gone to heaven. I thought he killed me. And you were St. Peter or Jesus or somebody come to show me the way to heaven. But now." She kissed him gently, licked his lower lip with her tongue. "Now I think it's a different kind of heaven you are bringing me to, Adamis. It is my honor to be your first. I want you to remember this for the rest of your life. When you are old and wrinkled and can hardly walk, I want you to think of this session and get so hard you could fuck me at 100 years old."

Adamis was having a hard time controlling himself. The visions she was painting were of course inaccurate, and how could she know after all, and would she feel this way or do this if she knew he was android and not human? She had no idea. And if he had sex with her, wouldn't it be under false pretenses?

He became worried that the abyss he was about to fall into would be something he could never recover from again.

He started to unwrap her hands behind his neck, and she moaned, "No. No, Adamis. You said he gave me to you. Tonight, you're going to give yourself to me. I own your body. I know you want this. Don't deny this for you or for me."

His mind was racing with all of the reasonable

things he could tell her, but, of course, he knew she wouldn't accept any of them. She'd more than likely be so angry she'd start a scene. She wouldn't be hurt as much as just completely angry, and this intimacy was something he wanted to experience.

There was no rule about his learning curve–he and Darius had talked about that. There were rules of society and rules that could land you in jail, and some of them would be broken here if he continued, but if they were both consenting and there was no force involved . . .

They washed and kissed. His fingers explored all the soft private parts of her body, he noted where she liked to be touched, and often she would hold his hand there. He felt her tender opening, he felt the soft lips of her sex and how she reacted when he pressed her there. She took his fingers and inserted them inside her, and then took her hand away and let him do it all his own, and he loved it. He loved every bit of it.

The kissing and fondling, even washing their hair together, relaxed him, but it also stimulated the part of him that wanted to show her how grateful he was that she was opening this doorway for him. It was nothing like what he thought he would experience. He knew he shouldn't, but he was going to allow himself the freedom that he'd been given, the freedom to love this woman in a way she deserved. He wasn't going to be able to do anything except what she told him to do. She would tell him how and where he should touch her, how to make her feel wonderful, and, in that process, he would feel wonderful too.

They dried off and, still slightly wet, retired to the bedroom. She pulled back the sheets and he found it difficult to slide inside still with the dampness on his body. She was beside him, tucked under his arm, and then she climbed over him, placing her palms on his shoulders, looking down into his face, and whispering, "This will change you forever, Adamis. Let me show you, let me help you . . . become a man. I don't know you except that I know you're good, and I know you want this, and I need to show you how much I appreciate your rescue. You are deserving of this."

Adamis had no words. Speech was just gone. He was in some kind of pink cloud that had taken over his whole body, every cell awakened and electrified just being next to this naked woman who was enjoying the feel of his body pressed to hers. She straddled his hips and reached down to place his member at her opening, drew herself up on one knee, angling her hip, and then seated herself on his member and pressed down all the way to his hilt. The incredible feeling of being inside this woman flooded him with an overload of emotions.

He thought he might burst a blood vessel or his heart would stop or something; he had never felt this way before. She watched him with a smile as she moved up and down his shaft, slowly, sweetly encouraging him as he lifted his hips to meet her body as he attempted with his hands to hold her down against him and go deeper.

It didn't take long before he understood exactly what it was she was asking. She was asking him to go deep, and he did. He gently pressed her to the limit to his hilt, he made her start to sweat and shatter, and, inside, some of her internal organs started to flutter, and she was almost to the point of being out of control, so she stopped and pressed herself against him, and then urgently raised and lowered herself several times and then stopped again each time he felt his engorged member getting larger, until, at last, something inside burst through and he filled her with his own fluids. He had ejaculated for the first time ever. And the feeling of being spent and bringing her to a point of orgasm was so thrilling he almost started to cry.

"Oh my God, Emmy. I never knew. I never knew."

"Shh. Be quiet now. I'm here. And you can have me as many times as you like. Let's do this all night long. Okay?"

He looked at her in astonishment. "How long do I–"

"I don't know. But let's try and see, right? That's the beauty of it, let's see how many times we can fuck before the sun comes up. Would you like that?"

"Oh my God, Emmy. Yes. Yes. I don't want this evening to ever end."

# CHAPTER 9

I T WAS NEARLY four o'clock in the morning before
Emmy finally collapsed and fell into a deep sleep,
snoring and drooling. And as Adamis looked down on
her in the light of the moon, he realized the graveness
of his feelings for her.

He should have been happy, seeing her so exhaust-
ed, satisfied, dreaming of a life and future that may
never come. But it broke his heart. And perhaps he had
put them both in danger because of his lack of control.

He'd never lost that control before. Was this coming from Darius' DNA, or was this something his own
body developed, nurtured and presented to him?
Something his brain thought he needed, and, without
instruction, delivered on that promise.

There was so much to learn about having a sexual
relationship with anyone, and it was never supposed to
be with a human, unless permission had been granted,
in advance. But, of course, Darius could fix that; it's

just that Adamis didn't want to place him in that kind of jeopardy, and he knew Darius would be upset, as he had every right to be. For these consequences affected him as well.

All the same, Adamis was an honorable man; he would do what he needed to do and face the reality of what he'd created. What he wouldn't allow is for something to happen to Emmy. Emmy had quickly become the trajectory that governed his immediate and urgent actions, and he was amazed at how fast everything had changed. He hoped he had the smarts to keep track of everything he had to keep track of to keep them both out of danger.

He slipped out of bed, brought his boxers into the living room, and closed the door behind him, hoping Emmy would sleep the rest of the night and not disturb him.

Inside the front coat closet was the safe where he kept his tablet from Darius. He quickly pulled it out, and checked for messages. It didn't appear there were any.

With some relief, he launched into his project. He signed into today and began sorting his thoughts. He would be careful how he communicated with his maker.

Tapping into the keyboard, he left Darius a message and requested a phone chat if that was possible. He told Darius there had been many things that occurred, and he had intended to call him earlier in the evening last night, but got distracted.

Adamis knew just spelling that out exactly as he did would alarm Darius, but it was the truth, and, if Darius was going to help him, he needed to know the reality and the truth of his situation.

It didn't take more than about 30 minutes before he heard the familiar beep and Darius was on the line, digitally.

*'Ready to communicate.'*

He dictated into the tablet's microphone, which would also leave a digital footprint and send a file to his internal records system, erasing the original message on the phone. It was a simple security element installed for his convenience. It was somewhat more complicated for Darius, as his brain didn't record and store data the same way.

"So I believe I have mentioned to you a woman, and I rescued her and brought her to my home in order to help with the healing and not involve the authorities. She appears to be nearly normal by now, which surprised me. I thought perhaps she had broken bones.

Her situation with the man is that he is basically a

scumbag, probably a low-level criminal who lives off the backs of women he turns into prostitutes. He gets them addicted to drugs. Emmy has admitted to this, although I have so far not seen any evidence of the addiction, but I sense she has used chemicals up until now.

If he comes after her, I will be forced to protect myself on a more permanent basis, as he is not a trustworthy person, and his knowledge of us together could cause both of us, all three of us actually, a problem. It somewhat pushes up my timetable to relocate since several other things have also occurred."

*'Very well. I got it. Continue, please.'*

"First, I want to let you know that Emmy showed me the wonders of sex last night. It's been in her conversation since the day she awakened in my condo. And this is the distraction I talked to you about earlier. I am grateful to her, and I believe she has honest feelings for me, which makes some of my decisions somewhat difficult to make. I want to know if I have the option of having her stay with me as I relocate, or if you don't approve of this. Does this place us in any additional danger or risk?"

*'Please continue. I'll answer this later after the rest of your communications.'*

"I visited the Security Chicks, and there is one of

them, Lisa, who has been accosted by one of her handlers, which turned into a full rape. She has told stories of hearing this happen to others, especially recently. Cherry also verified this.

They have asked for help, and basically there is none to be had. They've even inquired with female officers of the Emery City police force, and have been given nothing, and they were informed a few days ago that a prison ship will be docked next to their domicile, and it will be the Chicks' responsibility to become wardens of the ship. They're to ensure safety there and make sure that none of the prisoners who are brought in ever leave.

I can't say where it has come from, as the Chicks don't know very much, but they are clearly not only concerned, but scared. I was wondering if you'd heard anything about this, first. I promised I'd help them if I could, but needed to research, and that's the part that feels dangerous to me. Also, might there be someone you could put into place to help them, since I will be leaving? I don't want to delay my leaving, but I also don't want to go back on my word to help them. They are great allies, and I have learned so much from these ladies. I know I can trust them, not with everything, but with more than perhaps some of my other AI friends. You know what they say, a friend who is in need is a friend indeed. They need me."

*'Understood. Let me think on this. Is there more?'*

"I also stopped by the lab and chatted with Connor and Leon; I saw Emil, or what's left of him, de-parted, and it just reinforced my gratitude to you for having intervened on my behalf to make it possible for me to have a life outside of my life now. And that's I guess come full circle, so that my relationship with Emmy now becoming sexual is going to be a problem for me if I want to keep her protected.

My prime directive is to do no harm, to protect humans, and, secondly, to assist and protect other AI members of my community. But I have to tell you that it appears the human populations in this community are beginning to rise up against the androids, and I feel some kind of a war is brewing, perhaps a purge. Do you know anything about this?

I await your answer, as I'm sure you have lots of questions."

He got up to get a glass of water and was careful not to make noise when he brought ice out of the freezer. A few minutes later, he heard the familiar beep on the tablet.

*'First of all, Adamis, my son in every way except one, I'm pleased with your initiative, and you may think your report upsets me, but it actually confirms that you make good decisions on your own. I'm not sure about the woman, but it*

*seems like you did possibly save her life, and if she had died at the hands of the man and you had not acted quickly, stood by and watched, well that would've broken your prime directive and, to be honest with you, not many would trust you after that.*

*I know that women can be very charming, and my wife certainly was one of those. She never steered me wrong, however. She always put herself aside if it was in conflict with what I wanted or needed for my career. Your compatible companion would need to do the same, because you are going to have needs that perhaps she isn't aware of right now. And the magnitude of the promises you've made have perhaps impeded your progress. In any event, you need to catch up on your reading, you need to download the reports, and then you need to find a safe place for the notebook with all of the research and the references listed. You may need to relocate the storage facility. There will come a time when you may need that, and you'll see I've prepared some videos to be played at some future date for some future body that only would be necessary in the event that your life is threatened.*

*I don't know what you speak about when you talk about things changing, but it's been my estimation that things always change, and I don't see that slowing down anytime soon. Try to stay away from the hotheads and the trouble-makers. I give you permission to take out people who are by your definition the "scum of the earth." I just want to make sure you do it in such a manner that there is no paper trail, no film, no cameras, nothing at all. The way to do it is to make sure that they just disappear, almost like they disappeared on their own and had an accident and were never found again.*

*I don't want any getting even, no speeches, no letters left or manifestos. These people are not good people, and the changes you allude to are I believe a result of the fact that you AIs have done a better job than anyone expected running the world, or parts of it. Perhaps they are threatened. I do believe that some humans are jealous of this, and there may have to be some kind of war between the sides, before it gets better. So be prepared for that, and, by prepared, I mean get out of the way.'*

Adamis thought about what he just read. He needed clarification on one part of it.

"So is it going to be okay for me to take Emmy with me when I go?"

*'Are you able to leave her behind and know that she'll be safe?'*

"Not yet. How much time do we have?"

*'Not enough time, Adamis. If we are going to find someone to help with the Chicks' situation, it could take over a month for them to finish their research, and only then would the perpetrators be identified, and by then there may be a huge prison ship next door, which is going to change their entire lives, all of them. I'm wondering who the Emery police force will use in their place, as the Chicks have been very important to quelling the riots and dissatisfaction of the human population, and now, more and more, the AIs.*

*You're going to want to be long gone before that happens, otherwise they're going to ask you for help, and you can't do that. You're one person, and they have so much work ahead of them, that an escape for them will not be easy and will take a team. I will think about this a little bit and if I come up with something I will let you know, but you should probably let them know soon that you may have to take a small trip on my behalf and that your time is going to be limited, due to your duties for me. Tell them you'll get back to it later. I'm sure behind the scenes, if we set it up now, we can find somebody that can jump in. Do you have any recommendations?'*

Adamis thought about it. And then he considered Leon and Connor. Without waiting, Darius voiced his opinion.

*'I'd say Connor, although I don't think he wants the danger. Leon might be a better fit. I just don't know how committed he is to being selfless. He's going to have to stand up to a cabal of humans and androids who have been bought off, seeking to exert more and more control. That's what it seems like to me. I don't want you to get entangled in it, and we'll have to think twice before involving Leon or Connor. It's something we should know in a few days though.'*

"How were your tests? Are things still progressing but, hopefully, slow?" Adamis asked him.

*'If my wife were alive, she would give me some extra time. Just being around her made me feel healthy. She could cure me with her chicken soup, but it was her spirit, her love for me, that brought me forward, helped me walk over the coals in Hell itself. Do you know she was your biggest supporter in the beginning? Without her dedication, even though she knew very little of what we were working on, the project never would have come to fruition. You owe your life to her, in a strange way. I hope you don't mind the comment.'*

"That pleases me, Darius. But you are hedging.

How are the reports?"

*'The initial reports are not good, and it appears my cancer is growing.'*

"Surely there must be some way you can have a transplant, or obtain healthy organ tissue?"

*'Not exactly. I've never known anyone to do a brain transplant. Organs that you don't need, including fingers and toes and hands and arms and legs, are difficult but not impossible to live without. You can't live and possess a subhuman level psyche and brain pattern. It's going to be a difficult surgery for anyone who tries to do any kind of altering. And they have now instituted the parts inventory, which I'm sure you've heard about.'*

"Shocking, but, yes, I have."

*'I actually have an elderly woman acquaintance, an old friend of my mother's from years ago when the family lived in Virginia, and her android whom I was close to up until her death. I'm still trying to find him, but she's been put in the grave over a week ago now. My friends in the records office state that this Android is still very much alive, and may have gone rogue.'*

"So you've heard those rumors too. I thought it was just idle gossip. But there are those who have gone rogue?" Adamis asked.

*'Absolutely. No doubt about it. And the numbers are growing.'*

"The Chicks say that the San Francisco group is bringing in a special unit of AI, loaded with tactical capabilities, and, in addition to their handlers, who look and act more AI than most humans, they could be a significant force for quelling violence in the streets. Almost makes me think perhaps they know in advance something is coming. Do you feel the same way?"

*'God dammit, I was afraid of that. Now that whole new goon squad is going to be all over. You better stay away from the City, you should try not to shop more than you have to, and I think if you can't sell your condo then you need to gift it to someone.'*

"Can I gift it to Emmy? Can I just make a gift of the down payment and more? Or is that not allowed?"

*'I think you could gift it, but what I think is a bigger problem is the fact that we are quickly running out of time. You need to jump on this right away. Have you selected a place to go to?'*

"No, I'm sorry. Suggestions?"

*'If I were you, I would go to one of three places. The hills surrounding wine country in Healdsburg– there are little places tucked into the canyons there, places in the redwoods, places that are gated, and you could set up good security there. But it's not 100% safe. The second place I would think of would be down in San Jose on the way to the ocean at Capitola. In the Santa Cruz Mountains there are lots of small, tucked-away places. The problem with that is it's also highly populated, and that crowd is rather snoopy when it comes to who their neighbors are. I'm not sure that's going to work for you.'*

"So what's your third option?"

*'Some place near the ocean, either coast, but my suggestion would be anywhere along the South Carolina or Florida*

*coast, or perhaps the Gulf Coast region. Lots of sleepy towns with lots of strangers in and out from all over the universe. You'd fit in there. It's quirky.'*

This made Adamis laugh. He'd never heard Darius use that term, "quirky."

"Very well, I'll begin my research today. And, if I so choose, I have your permission to take Emmy?"

*'You do, but only if she wants to wholeheartedly. Otherwise, even though you may feel poorly about it, you'll have to leave her behind. You have the fate of lots of other AIs on your shoulders now, Adamis. Don't forget who you are.'*

He paused at this. Darius didn't sign off, indicating that he was probably giving him time to think. Then he asked his last question.

"How will all this work? Can you reveal the details?"

*'Well, I need to know first how soon and where you're going to move to, that you are ready and will be secure. Then I will have a medical incident, and I'll be put on life support and they'll come looking for you. So, when you hear I've been put on life support, that's your cue to get out of Dodge. That means you'll bring all the money with you, the credits, you'll bring all your notes, you'll have to leave behind the components of the warehouse unless you've moved them, because I doubt you're going to be able to go back there if something happens to me. But if you can transport it or do that quickly, which means, again, identifying where you're going to move, then you could save a lot of that material. The banking and funds, that's all electronic and it's all set up. You won't have any problem with that.*

*Now, with this twist of the new interest you have with this woman, well, I suppose it would be a safe cover to be traveling with her since they would never guess that you would be traveling with a woman. I would make sure that you not show her to any of your friends. I would do the best you can to try to hide it, and try to leave town in no later than a week. I am due for a checkup on Friday, and I've already got advanced notice that it's not going to be a good one. I won't be able to control it if he says I have to prepare for the worst, and, if that happens, everybody knows. That means I have to schedule your de-parting. If you're disappeared before that day comes, then I do believe you will be safe. I will make sure I tell people that it's already done and I have some extra components, things we took out during the last surgery that I can show as evidence that you are fully de-parted and will be no more.*

*But you understand, Adamis, if you show your face to any of the people who know you, your cover will be blown, as will mine. And while I only have a few weeks to live, your life of course will be terminated immediately. There are lots of dark things happening, and I think there are going to be lots of people needing you. Just hang in there, and remember who you are and what you stand for. In the face of disaster and war, everybody gets scared. Don't worry about that. What unusual and brave people and heroes do is they're scared, but they fight anyway. And they fight to win, they fight to hurt and to stop the enemy. You need to know that the enemy for us is anyone who stands in the way of our research, or takes advantage of other people, either humans or androids. Those are our enemies, and they need to be eradicated.'*

It was the first time Adamis' maker used those literal terms. He suspected that probably Darius knew more than he was letting on. But there was no judgment there, and he hadn't even had to tell Darius that he'd actually had sex with this woman. It was almost as if Darius already knew. And maybe, just a little bit, maybe he knew Adamis was going to need a companion. At least that's what he was going to go to bed thinking. For now, his biggest problem was going to be slipping into the sheets without waking Emmy. Because if Emmy woke up, he'd soon be very busy.

# CHAPTER 10

ALTHOUGH TIME WAS running out, Adamis didn't complain when Emmy woke him up, snuck under his arm, and began fondling him in places he found hard to resist.

"Good morning, Master of the Universe." She looked up at him, her hair tousled and her eyes full of desire.

Adamis felt an awakening in every single one of his cells, sparked by her taste, the scent of their lovemaking in the room, the little things he noticed about her that she didn't even know he saw, like the fact that her hair started to grow as she kissed him just infinitesimally, that the fine hairs on her body, her cheeks and her upper lip especially, stood to attention, almost begging that his fingers rub and touch them, press them down and let them spring back. She was fresh and young and supple, she wasn't electronic, she didn't have a keen sense of smell, sight–anything that he had–

but she had heart, she was human, she had a soul, and she was alive, truly alive.

As she rubbed against him, hugging his thigh by wrapping her legs around him, urgently riding him, he could hardly believe that this beautiful being who had so many other choices, had chosen to open herself completely, give herself to a machine, to a being who did not possess a soul, but who had instead a code of ethics.

But it wasn't the same thing, was it? She was truly alive, and Adamis was truly functioning. But, as far as having a life, a soul, he had all the things that made him imitate, like humans, but he didn't have the thing. He wasn't one of God's creations. He had been created by his maker, Darius. And Darius was far from being a god.

Whereas this woman was free to live, to love, to even make horrible choices with her life. Adamis was created for one function and one function only, to learn how to be more human, to keep humans safe, to save his brothers and sisters in the AI world, and to explore, keep growing, and possibly show humans how to live forever. It wasn't in the living that was important; it was in the teaching, the protecting, the creating the environment so humans could do their thing uninterrupted by other humans. There were in fact no evil AIs. There were AIs created by evil humans. And, yet, it was becoming evident, somehow the human population was turning on the AIs. Why?

As she kissed him, rubbing her nubile flesh against his, as she whispered in his ear things that he never thought a woman, especially a human woman, would ever say to him, these words of hers pouring out from her heart, he knew he did not deserve them, but he couldn't help himself. How could something that felt so affirming, so wonderful, be wrong?

She took pleasure and joy in telling him all these things without even knowing anything about him. She just wanted to please him and send him right up to the very edge of the branches of a very big tree. Where all the danger was, where he might fall and take her with him. And still he wouldn't be able to stop it or resist her desire for him. She was his gift, after all.

He hoped that she would answer some of his questions this morning in the positive. But for now, her mouth claimed him, her touch inflamed him, her scent drove him crazy with need. He wrapped his arms around her back and her quivering backside, lowering his hands to grab her buttocks with both of them, squeezing and then gripping to quickly flip her over on her back, placing himself over her, over her tiny wet opening which he had now learned how to do without using his hands. He placed his elbows and forearms on the bed sheets and silk pillow above her head. Trying not to pull down and entangle her hair further, he lifted her scalp and massaged it, kissing her neck, making her arch up to him so he could feel the taught nipples of her breasts press into his.

He paused, holding his member at the entrance to her womanness, felt it melt with desire and widen on its own to accept him, watching her panicked breathing and pheromones crashing over their bodies, and her little efforts to press him into her, and the deliciousness of his resistance.

Holding himself in check, he smiled down on her and she frowned, she moaned, and that was what he wanted to see. He wanted to see her face not having him, he wanted to see the evidence that she needed him so badly, he could tell her he was a machine and she wouldn't care.

Still, he wouldn't dare do that. There was so much more to explore. He'd find a way. Some day he'd find a way, he was sure.

"Please, Adamis, I need you inside me right now."

Her voice was hoarse, sexy as Hell, but on the wings of a whisper coming deep in her lungs. He still held himself at her opening, encircling her so that she knew how large and hard he'd gotten and would continue to get, all for her, all for Emmy and her beautiful body.

"I will go absolutely insane if you don't. I need what you give me; it's like an elixir that makes me feel wonderful. Please, please, I need you. Don't make me suffer."

He loved hearing those words and it made his heart swell, enjoying the pleasure of being caught between what he was going to give her, and enjoying the luxuriating feeling he would make her suffer to heighten her pleasure, and then plunge deep to give her the satisfaction they both desired. What a game this game of sex was! Why Darius had never told him about what this would be like, to totally invade someone else's body and system, bringing it to the edge of orgasm before he began to penetrate and persistently rammed home his lust, his love and his devotion to her and what they shared together.

He knew exactly what would happen as he entered her channel, that he would feel at home base, that he would fill her with seed that was not there. Fill her with his fluids and essence, but no spark of life, no commitment, except the one deep in his heart.

"Oh, Emmy, this is so magical. I never realized this could be."

"Adamis, please. Don't torture me any longer.

Please—"

As she arched up and closed her eyes, he thrust deep. He could not take his attention off her. He was transfixed, wishing in some kind of fantastic dream that this moment would last forever and ever. That there would never be any problems, that he never had a job that he didn't have to put himself in danger, or take her, whisk her away and keep her for himself in some secluded location, fucking day and night, never allowing her to dress, or shower, without him next to her, and never having to tell her the truth of it all.

Because none of this was supposed to happen, and humans were not allowed to spend eternity in a sexual relationship with AI beings. The world had made this rule, lived by that rule.

What if she said no to the move together, he wondered? He knew that he would not be able to resist being with her, and, if it meant he had to lie, well he would lie very well. He would convince her, make her feel loved because maybe he was learning how to do that after all. Maybe, the more and more he held her, felt her pulse under him, maybe it would become love. Maybe it had the power to transform not only her, but him as well.

His fingers moved inside her mouth. His cock was determined to drill a hole through the mattress, through the floor, all the way to the other side of the world. Their bodies melded and meshed, crescendoed, and at last melted into the sweat and the warmth of each other's arms, their kisses, both desiring not to see the reunion, the making of one from two lovers come to an end.

HE BREWED FRESH coffee and presented her with a mug filled with cream, just like she liked it, and asked her if she wanted something else since he had picked up eggs and milk and other things.

"I think we need about two dozen oysters, how about you?" She gave him a wry smile afterward.

"Oysters? I don't understand."

"You've never heard that oysters are good for especially men and their libido?"

"I never heard that. Of course, all I read are scientific journals. I'm not sure that would work with me." And then he stopped himself because he was about to tell her that oysters would have no effect on his body because he wasn't human. But, of course, he couldn't say that.

"I suppose it doesn't affect everyone the same way. So, what *is* good for your libido?"

"As you know, sweet Emmy, you're the one who has introduced me to all of this. So maybe we should buy some oysters. But today we have some other things we have to take care of first. But I'll try your oysters, and let's see where it takes us, okay?"

She had taken a long sip of her coffee, nearly spitting it out at his comment. "Oh, absolutely, I can't wait! If I told my friends that I'd spent the night with a man who made love to me, and I don't mean just made little bit of tiny love, you know, the little sweetness, kissing, hugging and nudging, I mean full on orgasmic love all night long, like ten times! They would never believe me. Now tell me, Adamis, if it isn't oysters, what is your secret?"

He sat down on the couch opposite her and sipped his coffee, peering over the top of his rim at her. He shook his head, "I have no idea. It just happened. I was overwhelmed with the feelings and the passion and maybe this only happens the first time."

"Oh my God, Adamis, no. That never happens. The first time, men always spew all over themselves, and it takes time to build their control. Sometimes I'd have to help them with that. I've been with so many men . . ."

And then she peered down at her lap. Her smile and angelic face turned into a grumpy one, and he could see shame written all over it. In a tiny voice, not exuberant, not confident, and certainly not happy, she said, "I'm sorry. I shouldn't have said that."

Adamis felt for her. He felt her pain and began to feel something else he hadn't expected, more of a telepathic capability between the two of them. He thought perhaps he could hear what she was telling herself. To experiment, he inserted a question without speaking, just to see if she could pick it up.

All of a sudden, she looked up at him.

"Did you say something?" she asked.

Overjoyed, he beamed and sipped his coffee, then tore his eyes away from her but couldn't stop smiling.

She jumped to her feet, came over and fell into his arms, almost causing him to spill the coffee all over both of them. He laid the mug down on the table and put his arms around her waist and let her tell him whatever in the world she wanted to. He would give her two or three minutes, maybe ten, before they had to get to work. But in those luscious five or ten minutes, he would let her fly like only she knew how to do. And she'd take him right with her.

"I'm so sorry about my past. If there ever was a man, and I don't know how I know this after only meeting you for three days—or four days has it been?"

"Four. If we want to be exact. But do we?"

"Do we? No! We don't want to be exact, do we! We want to be passionate and spontaneous and no rules, Adamis, no rules at all. No transaction of business, no money changing hands, just the way your heart," she said as she laid her palm against his chest. "Your heart against mine."

She took his palm and held it to her chest where he could not only feel her heart, but feel the electricity in her system, the way her brain was sparking and arcing; he felt the pain from last night's exertions, the little redness of her opening, the need she still had in her belly, the smoothness of her skin and the desire to dream, to fly, to escape this world that he used to think was perfect.

But now, what was perfect was in danger.

"It means little to me, Emmy. I don't care about what your past is. I need what you have and are right now. And maybe your past is something that happens so that you could appreciate what you have today. But it doesn't matter. Don't worry, don't spend any time worrying about what I feel about it. You opened the door for me, you brought me to a different world that I never knew. And for that, I will be eternally grateful."

"And I never want to leave you, Adamis. Tell me, please, that if you move, if you travel, you'll take me with you. Please take me with you."

So there it was.

He didn't even have to ask. He'd learned two things this morning, well three probably. The first one was he would never be able to live without her. The second one was she didn't want to be without him. And three, he loved having sex with her and planned on never ever having sex with any other woman for as long as he was alive. He would care for her, he would cherish her, he would protect her at all costs for all time.

Whatever that precise thing meant. It didn't matter.

# CHAPTER 11

ADAMIS REVIEWED SOME of the places he was considering, based on the suggestions that Darius had made. It didn't take him long before he realized that the further away from the Bay Area probably the better it was going to be for him. Unlike perhaps other AI beings, it wasn't important for him to be near a big center that specialized in AI development, parts or even research. He was supposed to take care of things on his own. And that was the real test.

He looked up at Emmy, who was reading a magazine she'd picked up downstairs in the lobby. He wondered how she had fared with the security guard down there.

"Emmy, I want to ask you a question."

"Sure, go ahead."

"Where was your most favorite place that you've ever lived?"

"Lived or vacationed?" she asked.

"Lived, as in you thought it was a nice place to grow up, to shop, I suppose it matters what age you were. But I'd just like to know what your favorite was, and why."

"My parents, when they were together and before all the darkness, the drugs and everything, they took me to Disneyland one time. I thought I'd gone to Heaven. It was magical, really magical. I didn't realize that there could be a whole place that was created, it wasn't real, but it was like a fake city, a fake village and a fake community. All with mechanical beings and special rides and cars and people that dressed up in costumes and oh, my gosh, it was such a wonderful place to get lost in. It made me forget that we lived in a dumpy house, that my dad drank too much, and my mom was unhappy, crying all night long. I was taken with the fact that this stage, this large play was all laid out before us. None of it real, but looking and feeling real. I did feel like I lived there, and, years later, I would dream about it."

It wasn't the answer he'd expected from her. She was looking for a place that wasn't real, but looked real? Wasn't that an apt description of the person she was sleeping with now? And wasn't it more merciful she didn't know the difference, just like as a child she could enjoy living in the Magic Kingdom where everything always turned out beautiful and there was a Happily Ever After for her. Something, so far, she'd never experienced.

He was moved by the promise that perhaps he could create that for her somehow. She did deserve it.

Emmy continued, "I always wanted to go to Disney World in Florida, but we never got there. We often looked at pictures of that weekend in L.A., and saw advertisements of happy families in Florida, walking on the beach with Mickey Mouse. After awhile, I couldn't look at those ads because it was too painful. I felt like an outsider looking through a glass cage at all the real families having the time of their lives, enjoying themselves without any of the fear that gripped my life. And that was when things were good. As you know, they got worse. When my parents got sent away, I didn't really miss them. I missed the pictures that were thrown out when the house was returned to the bank, and all the contents squished like garbage. Why would my uncle let me see that?"

Adamis knew. "He didn't want you to think there was a way out, that there was a home to come back to. You already knew there was no family. He had more control over you that way."

"Yeah. You're right. That's exactly what happened. I lost control over myself, depended on others, the drink, the drugs, all done to make my dreams fade away."

She was crying when he hugged her again. "You're safe now. Remember what I told you that first night? You have nothing to fear now that I am here. I won't let anything hurt you."

"You are a miracle, Adamis. A true miracle."

He held her for a few minutes and then asked, "What about vacations other than your trip to Disneyland. Are there any places that you've seen that you'd like to visit?"

"One of the girls moved to South Carolina. She actually married one of our johns, and you know, for a prostitute, that's always the wish or the hope, but she was different, and she was probably always looking for a way out, whereas the rest of us I think we had given up after the beatings and the brutalization. I liked taking those drugs and I did that instead of trying to plot getting away, but she got away. She sent me a postcard once that showed a beautiful white sand beach. I think if I could go anywhere I would go there, or maybe more south. Key West?"

Adamis considered her answer, and started searching the southern East Coast. He found several small communities between St. Augustine and Fort Pierce, Florida; he also looked over the Miami area and immediately saw lots of possibilities there. But he also was concerned about the influx of so many people and the creation of large cities on the beach. Cities were one caution Darius had given him. Maybe the higher population would put him in the same kind of danger that being in a large city like San Francisco or Emery City would afford them. He started looking for sleepy little beach towns.

He also searched industrial spaces and came across a warehouse complex that had been put into bankruptcy, just outside of Tampa, good access to the airport but was in an area that perhaps had gone downhill and was in need of redevelopment. There had been a stadium deal that failed, and they'd lost a number of sports teams, so all of a sudden this huge complex and acreage was available for a very good price.

He studied it and the pro formas of the project for several minutes, and then he ruled it out. He was concerned about the many City Council meetings he'd have to endure, the public hearings on the use of the land, due to the high profile nature of it. It would require a ballot initiative and rezoning if he could develop a lab/research facility. Too many people looking over his shoulder, asking too many questions he didn't have answers to. He needed housing for the people he wanted to bring with them. He wanted a place for them to be able to work, do research unfettered.

Out toward the Gulf of Mexico he found a few towns that were within an hour of the beach that had stores or shopping centers and malls that had gone out of business. One was a wholesale food distributor and it had a massive warehouse that came with refrigeration and a ton of space for storage. In fact, the inside could be remodeled into a very efficient and enormous lab if he wanted. There also was the possibility that they could have their electricity generated by solar or wind, and that would greatly reduce the cost of ownership.

If he sold his condo, he could pay cash for the building; if he didn't have that time, he would need to get terms. And that wouldn't include buying a house. He was going to have to contact Darius, and let him know what he was thinking.

"What about you, Adamis?"

He'd forgotten she was still sitting there with him.

"I'm of the same opinion; I think we should think about areas as far away from California as possible. And I like the idea of being close to the ocean, don't you?"

"I do. I think being closer to the beach is something that anybody would love. And we could have a boat,

Adamis, we could go sailing. Or we could sail or travel to the Caribbean. Some of those countries are just now recovering from the wars that broke out mid-century. I think they'd be good places to go as well."

He thought about it all, and very carefully too.

Emmy was getting stir-crazy, and begging for an opportunity to get outside. Adamis wasn't going to reveal everything about his concerns with the front desk, but he asked her about her takeout order and her ability to get the magazines she had.

"So did they give you any trouble when you got the takeout order?" he asked her.

"Well, it was already charged to you, I don't know, the delivery person was at the desk when I went down to pick it up."

"Did you have to sign the register?"

"No, I was just picking up the food. I signed the bill from the delivery person, but I signed your name. I didn't know what your last name was so I just signed it Adamis. And I had to guess at that. I probably misspelled it. I took it upstairs and on the way I saw a shelf of magazines and I asked the desk if I could take a couple and he agreed."

"That's amazing. Did he know you were staying in my place?"

"No, I don't believe so. If he checked with the delivery person he would see the signature, but, no, he didn't ask me any questions at all. I guess I looked like I lived here, right?"

"You do now."

He thought about telling her a bit of the truth of their situation. Maybe it was time, and maybe it would keep her inside, waiting for him.

"One of the things I need to let you know is that there have been some recent changes that have gone on, and when I came in this time they had me sign a sheet. There are some rules and there's a new owner-ship of this complex ground floor, if you can believe such a thing, and based on that they're going to be a lot more strict about the going and coming. That's one of the reasons why I've decided not to live here any longer."

"I see. So this is recent, then?"

"Yes, and I was rather upset by the way I was treat-ed, as if, as a paying resident of the complex, for some reason they were looking for some kind of an excuse to move me out. I don't know for sure that that's the fact, but I don't feel safe and I don't feel welcome any longer. And now with you, Emmy, I don't feel safe for that reason as well."

"Do you think it has to do with the fact that I'm here? Do you think they could possibly know?"

"I don't think so. But if they wanted to check, you know there are cameras everywhere, I hope not here–"

Emmy put her hand up to her mouth. Then she started to giggle. "Oh my God. What they're going to see if they have a camera in this place. Oh, we've been so bad, Adamis. If they find that recording, those guys aren't going to get any work done for days. They'll be watching that thing over and over and over again!"

She went back to perusing her magazine, and Adamis sent a communication to Darius. The reply he got was instant.

*'I have two days only, so I will send the funds to you in the next thirty minutes. Put in your offer on the Florida property you sent me. It's perfect. If you want, I can facilitate the relocation of the lab to that address, and put it under my shell, DJ Land and Cattle Co. I suggest you tie it up tonight, and offer them a sizeable deposit as earnest money, something they'll not be able to refuse. Offer to close it within ten days—that will get their attention.'*

"Shouldn't I go check it out first?"

*'We don't have time. Remember, if they determine I'm to be hospitalized, I have no say in the matter. Even I will have no say in the matter. That's the point of no return. You buy it, and anything you need to do, you do after you own it. See if you can meet and gather a group of you together.'*

"Roger that. I'm on it. Thanks, Dad."

Adamis hesitated afterward, wondering if he should have called him that. Darius quickly answered.

*'I've been waiting a lifetime to hear that. Yes, you are my son, and I am your dad, in a father-son relationship that is now coming to an end. But don't grieve for me. Put all your energies into the rest of your life. All my notes, all my love and best wishes are with you, my son.'*

"Thank you, Dad. I love you."

And then Darius left one more text. *'Almost forgot, I found someone for Cherry and the girls. He will instruct them to contact you when it's all done. But they'll be protected. Maybe you can start a harem, who knows?—Dad'*

Then it finally happened. He felt moisture in his eyes, but not quite enough for a tear.

# CHAPTER 12

ADAMIS WAS PREPARING to leave to pick up the cell phones from Cisco. Emmy, of course, wanted to go with him, and he made her promise that she would stay put for now.

"I don't know what's going to happen when I come back in and get interrogated by the security guard in the lobby again. The number of times I leave and go back has to be cut drastically short. Like I said yesterday, I want to be done with this quickly. I also have some other banking to do and I think you're going to be pleasantly surprised when I get back and let you know what I've contracted to purchase in Florida."

"You bought something?" She asked.

"No, but I have made an offer. I used a proxy to put in an offer on a property in Florida. I think you're going to be happy with it. I also have a few things I need to take care of and I have to check in with a couple of my friends. So I will be back, within an hour or two at the most." He stepped toward her and gave her a hug. "Do you need anything? Should I pick up something?"

"We still have some of the leftover tamales and the sausages I was making the other day; I have eggs and plenty, really. We have coffee. I don't think so. Just hurry back, please. I'm going to be filled with worry while you're gone."

"Well, part of what I'm going to fix is that issue. I'm going to get a cell phone that we can communicate on, something that won't be traced. Everything I do now on the AI network is reviewed and possibly traced, which exposes both parties. I'm trying to eliminate as much of that as possible. So this will help. You and I can speak more freely even when I'm not here."

"I understand. I'll be here. I'm not going any-where."

"And in case someone comes to the door, do not answer it. If you have any electronics on–actually, I think it would be best if you don't turn anything on. I think you should just be quiet, and read, sleep. You surely must need some of that, right?"

"You wear me out. But I love it."

He kissed her on the cheek and she grabbed him and kissed him full on his lips, making it difficult for him to extricate himself from her.

At the bottom of the elevator, Adamis checked himself and his demeanor; he straightened his hair and adjusted his clothes so that he was all business. He also masked his thoughts in case anyone with enhanced telepathy was out there, and put on a pair of reading glasses that he thought might help disguise his leaving the building. As he rounded the security desk, he waved without looking for the person, and heard someone clear his throat, as if he'd been sleeping and then suddenly awakened. He did not want to turn to check it out.

On the street, he did enjoy the freedom of the air, especially the moist, salt air from the San Francisco Bay, the sounds of traffic and sea birds, airplanes above and tiny personal helicopters that buzzed around like bumblebees. He headed over to the lab across the Bay, and met Connor at the doorway.

"So what have you been up to?" Connor asked him. Adamis noticed he was completely blocking the doorway.

"Is something wrong?"

"Fuck, no. But I got bad news. Remember we were talking about all that stock and digital currency scam that was going on, remember a couple of days ago when you came by?"

Adamis realized he was using code for the discussion they'd had about the police in San Francisco. "Yes. Don't tell me you made an investment?"

"No, I stayed away, but these darn salesmen, you know how direct and difficult they can be. I'm not good at pushing them off. They don't take no very well for an answer. I'm sure you understand." He looked directly into Adamis' eyes to make sure his message was delivered.

Not having the telepathy with Connor made it difficult to communicate nonverbally.

Adamis approached it another way. "Would you like to sit down and hear my side of things or my opinion about what's going on?" Adamis asked him.

"Let me check first." Connor opened the door a sliver and Adamis could hear the sounds of a heated discussion. There was somebody else in the room who was making a big to-do about the body parts belonging to their former library tech. Apparently Emil's head didn't arrive, nor the rest of the parts the Manhattan Library had requested. Adamis looked through the doorway despite the metal shielding that was intended to keep prying digital eyes out and was able to make out the faint bluish outline of a very heavyset man in a trench coat, and he smoked a cigar of all things. That put him in a different category according to Adamis, meaning that he was a member of organized crime.

Local politicians and police were generally not heavyset–nor smokers–because it was deemed to be untrustworthy if they were, and they also didn't speak so bluntly, so loudly with that guttural accent from somewhere. Adamis immediately saw what Connor was in the middle of.

He was grateful his friend didn't want to get him involved.

Adamis walked around the corner and waited in the shadows, listening for the door to open again so he could resume his conversation. He waited nearly 30 minutes, and then a flock of pigeons, flew up into the air just before he heard the slam of the metal door of the warehouse.

He heard someone call out, "Hello?" and he recognized it as Connor's voice.

He walked back to the entrance and greeted his friend. "I can see you have your hands full. So what's all this about?"

Connor searched the alleyway both to the right and the left; he even checked the tops of the buildings across the street. In a whisper, he said, "Inside, please. Keep your voice low."

Adamis followed Connor inside. Leon was laying on the floor covered in blood, but when Adamis came over to him to check his vitals, determined that he'd just been knocked out and didn't sustain any real injury, except he would have a black eye and perhaps a very sore jaw. The cut over his eye had already clotted with his bluish purple serum that was his blood. His pulse was strong, his circuits were fluttering a bit, but nothing other than the shock of landing on the floor. He decided to let him revive on his own rather than bringing him to consciousness. He figured his body would do a better job over anything he could do.

"So who was this guy?" he asked Connor.

"Lali Mustafa. He deals in body parts, android body parts. He's a black marketeer. Apparently Emil's body was supposed to go to the Manhattan Library, but, as you know, they wanted his head, because it had all the data in it about, you know, the books and everything. None of his parts arrived in Manhattan and it's a shit storm. They're blaming us. The Security Department heads in Emery, San Francisco and even Manhattan have already been here, and they've threatened to shut us down if we don't find where Emil went to."

"Don't they understand there's a big market in body parts, especially AI body parts?"

"Oh, they understand, all right, they just don't care. They don't care who they have to intimidate or kill, they are out for blood. I'm telling you, Adamis, this is not sustainable. We can't live like this forever."

He hesitated. Playing back his last conversation with Darius, he weighed his risk of letting Connor know about his plans.

"What if I told you maybe there's another way. Would you and Leon be ready?"

Connor leaned very close to Adamis' ear. "In a hot minute," he whispered. The two men stared at each other for a few seconds, and then Connor added, "Are you serious? Are you going to make the jump?"

"I'm not sure I have any choice."

"Nor do I any longer, it seems. What about Darius? He would be heartbroken."

Adamis didn't say a word, just stared back at his friend. Finally, Connor's head began to nod, slowly at first, and then he gave Adamis a wink. "I get it now. And when will this be?"

"Yesterday I would've told you a week or two. Today I'm telling you as soon as you can. I'm going to be arranging to do private research for Darius, which will require that I transport to the East Coast. I'm not at liberty to say yet, but are you with me?"

"Absolutely. I got nothing here. And I don't think I have much time either. What the hell is going on?"

"I don't have it verified yet, but Darius seems to think there is a purge going on perhaps. Perhaps not. But everybody's being replaced who is halfway reasonable or easy to work with. They're bringing in half-breeds, half-Android/half-human, altered humans basically. And the AIs they're bringing in are ruthless with no feeling or personality. They'll do anything. They'll sacrifice themselves like they have no skin in the game. I talked to Security Chicks; they're basically being disbanded, being driven off the Emery Police force payroll and now they're going to be wardens for a prison ship coming into the bay very soon. Their new job is going to be taking care of that crowd. Can you imagine that? I mean, those girls were the best tacticians. The *best* of us."

Connor stared at the ground. "Gosh, it's times like these I'm so glad I'm not human. I'm glad I don't have a wife or children or anything like that. I just have my friends. I have no baggage. I don't own anything, I don't have any money, and all I got is my safety. I mean, you and I, we don't have a life, do we? All we have is a future, a future that we thought we had. And, now, we're watching it all being taken away bit by bit. The respect, the jobs, you know we haven't seen a new de-parted come through here since Emil? It's like all of a sudden we have a leper colony here or something. Nobody's coming. Nobody calls. I get the feeling that if we were just gone one day, nobody would care."

"What about your handlers?"

"Well, that's the thing, Adamis, I haven't been able to reach mine in two days. They told me he had to go in for a medical procedure? And nobody knows where he is. I mean, I can't even get hold of his wife; nobody knows where he is at work. I've left messages."

"That's curious. That's never happened before, has it?" Adamis asked him.

"No. God, I wish I had all your faculties; you sure you don't know anything? Maybe it's just my creepy mind doing a digital flush or something, I don't know. Maybe my circuits are burning out or something. Could I just be making all this up? Maybe I need an oil change."

Adamis laughed, placing his hand on his friend's shoulder. "Connor, I think you're one of the most sane men on the planet. You never complain. You do your job, and you do it perfectly. Oh, we gossip, but we did that because we felt we had the freedom to express ourselves. We felt untouchable, had an existence with few cares and little danger."

"That was then. This is now, Adamis. I'm scared. For the first time in forever I'm really scared."

"There must have been a reason they sent Emil to you, and asked you to ship him out. Maybe they didn't want anyone else to know he was gone or being departed. And now that he's lost, well, they have the perfect opportunity to come back to you, don't they? And isn't that something punishable by death? Losing an AI body part? A whole AI person?"

As Leon began to stir and slowly get himself up off the floor, examining the blood on his fingers after he touched his forehead, noting the cut there, Connor continued.

"Death? Is there such a thing for us? Don't we just go away somewhere? Don't we de-part? Wind up living the rest of our lives in other people's bodies? There is no death for us, Adamis. It would be punishable by death if we were human, but we're not. We're expendable. And there's nobody to stop them. Maybe we could have. But we were too busy focusing on our jobs."

"I say we change all that. I say we even the odds and start fighting back to gain some control over our lives—something we really never had in the first place. But, Connor, we've earned it. We've been paying our dues since the day we were created, haven't we?"

# CHAPTER 13

ADAMIS HAD TO hurry to make his appointment with Cisco on time. As before, the man sat in the corner, the darkest part of the restaurant, drinking a beer. Adamis waved to Cisco's mother and leaned into the kitchen window to let her know how much they had appreciated her tamales.

"You want to take more home tonight?" she asked.

"Absolutely. I think they were the very best I've ever tasted."

"I'm glad. I'll prepare another six for you then."

Adamis returned to the dark corner and sat across the table from Cisco. "I apologize for being late. I had a little incident with a couple of my friends, and, well, I had to take care of some duties for work, give them a hand with something. Things are sure getting crazy around here."

"Yes. I agree completely." He leaned forward on the table just as he had the other night. "Adamis, I hope you realize what you mean to your community as well as to those of us who understand who you are and what you are about. You realize you actually have quite a bit of power when it comes to community events?"

"No, that's all Darius. That's not me. I just do what I'm told."

"I think that's not completely the truth, my friend, and you know it. You've been told to be humble, and, while I can appreciate that, Adamis, you have to understand that you probably better than anyone are in a position to help this community, perhaps to help the whole country or the world. These are very strange times as you said. And I'm not so sure the good guys are winning."

"You know that my directive is never to cause harm to any human being. Unless they're causing harm to others or to my brothers and sisters. And it's a very thin line that separates the two. With recent edicts and changes coming down the pike—"

Cisco interrupted him. "That's what I'm talking about. Everything that you used to be able to do, they are taking that away. They are making it harder and harder for you, me, for all of us, just regular people, making it harder for us to survive. You have to protect yourself because we need somebody we can believe in. We need somebody who's stronger and more capable to help us fight."

"Cisco, I'm well aware of what your background is and how you make your money."

Before he could continue, Cisco interrupted again. "But it's only illegal because they made it illegal. It should be an open marketplace. I should be able to deal in untraceable cell phones. I should not be hampered in doing this. It shouldn't be black market stuff. It should be out in the open, just like any legitimate store."

He made a good point.

"Look at the service I provide. Look at the people who need that anonymity, who need to do things maybe a little bit outside the lines or who don't trust the people who are supposed to be watching the pot. They make rules and laws so fast it's impossible to fight them because they have the power of the laws and the police and the military. We are just trying to live our lives. And they're sucking the blood, the stuff, the guts out of us. You do see that, don't you?"

Adamis was grateful for Cisco's perspective and for his respect, but he wasn't ready to take up arms or fight in any overt way.

"Cisco, you and I agree on all of this. But, right now, I'm fulfilling an order, a wish for my maker, call it if you will a last rite of passage? I am doing this for

Darius. And, in a strange twist of fate, Darius is doing this for me. He has commanded me to move on."

"I guessed as much. So he's going to set you free?"

"I never told you that and I will deny it if someone accuses me of saying so. But I am moving, at his suggestion, and with his blessing. And I need to be able to communicate with those I trust without scrutiny."

"Good. That's good. Because I have a proposal for you. I would like to be your contact person to the rest of the world. Maybe you don't trust Darius, or maybe Darius has too many eyes on him, or—"

Adamis raised his eyebrows and let it sink in. After several seconds, he saw the expression change on Cisco's face, the recognition that Darius was leaving this world. And he didn't want to take Adamis with him.

"Oh my God. Then you are the one who needs to be protected," Cisco surmised.

"No, I am the protector. I need to be left alone, un-fettered; I need to set some things in motion, and then I'll be in a better position to help others. But your offer of staying in communication, that's very real and of great value to me. I know many AIs whom I also trust. But—other than Darius—I believe you, Cisco, and I believe you want to help. I just don't want to be re-sponsible for you or your family if something happens and your help for me backfires and you wind up having to pay the price. That wouldn't be fair. Right now this is my war, or what I thought initially was going to be my adventure. I was so excited to be striking out on my own, and test Darius' handiwork, test my own theories, grow and develop and learn everything I could about humans and maybe just maybe I could find a way. But if I have to resist and fight, well that's going to take an army, isn't it?"

"Now you know the real reason Darius is setting you free. The world needs you in this state, not departed and transplanted into others, not in a box in a warehouse somewhere, being picked over by parters looking for a cheap addition to their service bot. He wouldn't want that for you."

"But I am no leader, Cisco. No General. I'm not a politician or a military man."

"You are my capitan. You could lead my squad any day. I have a network of mostly teenagers, some elderly, no AIs. But we see it. We see the day of reckoning as coming. They are trying to control everything, and the one group that they cannot truly control is the AI community. They're afraid of you, Adamis. They're afraid you're smarter, that you could take over."

Adamis smiled, remembering some of the books he had read, books Cisco wouldn't begin to know about.

"Yes, I understand. Little men. They fear in others their own flaws. They fear most what is most present in them in their own personalities. They project their shortcomings onto us. They're afraid of us and yet, if we work together like I thought we were for years, we could solve most of the world's problems. But, instead, what they seem to be doing is jockeying for control, trying to shut down all the avenues of escape, trying to make meaningless all the best parts of our society. The invention of our AI brethren and the extensive use of the AI community has furthered the advancement of humans as well as AIs. It was a good gesture, it was a good decision. But, now, instead of being courageous, they're being small, they're being afraid, they're fighting over turf instead of organizing, working together and tackling all the problems of society, problems they've partially caused themselves. I never saw it this way until I talked to several people this week. I always had unresolved questions but it wasn't until I started to listen, really listen, as I was preparing to say goodbye, that I saw for the first time all the need and the pain and suffering that was so unnecessarily caused. I can help but I can't help right now."

Cisco leaned over and tapped Adamis' hand, grabbing his fingers. "Enough. Enough. I have what you asked for, and you in return need to do something for me."

"Name it."

"I'm going to give you several phones, a whole box of them. Practically my entire stash. I want you to give them out carefully. They're without trackers so they can't be traced back to me, but I want you to give these phones, this old technology, to several people you trust. And I would like you to make me the point of contact. They can perhaps message you, but I would like you to use me as a conduit, as a leader of your supporters. And, when the right time comes, and you call me, I will join you. In the meantime, I will keep your comms straight and I will collect more for whomever you designate as being worthy. We will build a network, Adamis. A network consisting of old ways, old parts, old systems that worked for generations. We will find a way to find their weakness, and, far from destroying them, we're going to try to save them, whether they want it or not."

"You are a brave man, Cisco."

"But listen to us. Isn't that crazy? We save them, and they are afraid of us?" he said as he wrinkled his nose.

"I think every inventor, every visionary, every student of humans understands that you have to be a little bit crazy to move forward. For every hundred people who say you can't do something, there's one who says you can, and that's the one you partner with. You don't listen to the hundred, you listen to the one."

"You are the one, Adamis," Cisco said again, squeezing his hands, his gnarled and scarred fingers making a bowl of knots out of their hands in front of them. "You are the one, because you don't know how to let people down."

Cisco picked up a wooden box, a large crate about the size of two reams of paper, with a lid on it that slid open. Inside, Adamis saw several phones. Some had colorful plastic covers, some had stickers with daisies and giraffes and smiley faces. It was obvious that all these phones came from mostly humans who had lives that were now gone. And yet the old technology was still alive and still able to be used. The cell towers had to work because they still used cell towers in certain forms of communication, especially for air travel, and, with the switch over to satellite networks, they also fed into these old towers. The old phones had all been adapted and were still in use, up until the time of their owner's death. Adamis looked at the box of phones like the biggest treasure trove he'd ever seen.

Cisco slid the lid back, covering the jewels he'd found, and handed him the box.

"Inside I have a piece of paper with my number on it. You call me, text me, and we'll have our means of communication. Very simple, impossible to track. For the others, they push the large button in the bottom and it will tell you what the phone number is. Again, these are not traceable. You let me know and then you will have access to all the people using these phones."

"Do you know what you've just given me?"

"A box of phones. A box of old phones. Junk to most people."

"No, Cisco, you've given me hope. Maybe we can do this. This, my friend, is a box of freedom."

# CHAPTER 14

PREPARING HIMSELF FOR the eventual confrontation with his condo's security guard, Adamis purchased a pair of gloves and a scarf, enhancing the story that he was cold. It had been a rainy day. He didn't want to risk bringing his DNA to nefarious operators who might be collecting all the residents' markers. He now suspected part of the reason for it was to identify who in the condo complex was human and who was AI.

There was no other logical reason for it. He didn't think that he as a person was a person of interest, and there was no reason for them needing to identify all the individuals in the complex, because there was a list on file, created when each of the units sold. Monthly homeowner statements were sent out, so they would know if anything had changed.

But, if the new owners were not the ones sending out these statements, or somehow the security team had been compromised, maybe there was a different agenda—perhaps a much larger one than just keeping track. Could they be part of the cabal attempting to purge the city, as some of his AI brethren thought, as Cisco thought? And then perhaps the state, perhaps the country? They would start small, one building at a time, and, before it was commonly known, would spread beyond what anyone could control.

And that could mean, any AI who is living amongst human beings anywhere could be in danger.

Adamis chastised himself for bringing up demons perhaps his own mind created, or was it their hive mind that had yet to be created? Had the people in positions of power in the human population become distrusting of their creations, wanting back what they perceived as a giveaway of their power? But how would he know for certain? Had they all made this up? Was Adamis guilty of leading others off a cliff of no return?

*'Trust yourself ... trust who you are. Remember, Adamis, why you were created ...'*

The haunting words from his father, from his maker, came back to him. Darius was right. There wasn't anything other than to trust the instincts that were growing with each and every encounter, each and every day. Maybe this was even a sense of precognition, something humans would never have. It almost felt like that.

He entertained thoughts and images of the Security Chicks, isolated and floating on a big boat, all of a sudden being relegated to staying put, not performing their fantastic feats of rescue and safety, of criminal apprehensions and protecting the lives of their handlers. No, they were to take on a lesser job, a job where they could be monitored, watched, and, one by one, as their makers retired from this world, they'd be reparted, their parts sold off to the highest bidder, or perhaps they'd be bought and sold on the black market or by owners who needed the money.

There were all kinds of things Adamis could imagine now that he'd spoken to his friends.

As he walked past several shops on the way to the building, he noticed news reports of unrest in San Francisco, more in Sacramento and Los Angeles. These were huge violent crowds of people with banners, some wearing masks, war paint, mimicking those protests he'd seen accounts of at the turn of the century, and later, now growing in violence. And with these came the violent reaction of police forces, trying to quell the riots, people crying out for protection from every brutal corner of these once-great cities.

But the protection they needed was to be made free from those who organized and those who pitted themselves brutally against these protestors. Adamis had a theory brewing that these two groups could in fact be one organized effort to sow widespread chaos and tear apart the fabric of society they'd learned to live with. He'd not considered this a possibility.

Maybe he should violate his own rules and look into what kind of demographics and what the crime statistics were in Florida. But then he realized it didn't matter. What he was going to do was just going to be private, and as far away from Silicon Valley or San Francisco as possible. He hoped this movement, if it was that, hadn't yet spread to the rest of the States of Unity. Formerly called the United States, Adamis preferred to use the old term.

He hadn't even tried to create it, but a network had formed almost by itself around him. He was a leader amongst a group of AIs and a few humans. If they ever got together, that would be the day, wouldn't it?

He wondered what Emmy would think if she saw this tiny network of freedom fighters, fighting in ways he never thought possible.

He entered the lobby, and a new bored and sleepy-looking gentleman in the same blue and gray colored uniform gruffly greeted him.

"You will kindly sign in," he said in a completely monotone voice. "Please, sir," he added as he pointed to the clipboard on the desktop.

"Of course." Adamis started to take out his pen and the gentleman gave him a quick rebuke.

"No, no, no, not that pen. You must use my pen. The ink has to match," the gentleman said, thinking Adamis was dumber than he was. It made no logical sense at all.

"I understand," he lied. And then he smiled.

It hadn't happened yet, but he knew one of these days he would have to put down his apartment number, but for right now he could sign his name, show his identification papers, including his international passport certificate, and then he was allowed to go home.

As he headed to the elevator, it struck him how odd it was that he had to show papers just to go home. He had to show papers to work, he had to get a license if he wanted to ever drive a vehicle, which he had never done–but to go home? He had to have a pass to get into the building at the Adam Group, but just to walk in and change his clothes and take a shower and watch something or listen to music, he had to show his identification just to do that? It had all changed so fast.

The elevator doors opened and he pushed the button to the 16th floor.

Emmy was delighted to see him. He held up the tamales. "We have tamales again, and my friend's mother says she's grateful that you liked them."

After her hug and kisses, she said, "Adamis, some-day I'd like to thank her personally. Do you think I'll be able to do that soon?"

"Of course, we'll work on that, maybe not soon, but, yes, we'll do that," he lied. He lied because in Adamis' fantasy world, his magic kingdom, that was possible. He could see it happening, he could see the clip playing in his brain, the happy reunion, how Cisco's mother would wrap her arms around Emmy, and Emmy would give her a kiss perhaps. It was all possible, but not today, maybe not even next year. But it was possible, and, as long as it was possible, it was real, as real as it could be.

They sat for a quick dinner and then he took a shower, putting on his flannel pajamas, slipping on his blue, wool slippers, and then snuggled on the couch with Emmy.

"So? You said you bought something. I want to see it," she implored.

Adamis got out the tablet from the coat closet safe. "There's one thing I have to say first. Emmy, this tablet is very special. It is never to be touched when I'm not here. I keep it in a safe place under lock, but it is a lifeline to what we need to do to get out of here. So treat it as my most valued possession. And don't ever violate the space or try to hack into it or use it. It will lock down, and all the information stored there will be lost forever. It's critical that I have it. Do you understand?"

She nodded solemnly, "Where did you get that?"

"It's for my job. You know I have a very important job, and I can't talk about it, only to say there are things that are sacred to me, and you have to promise not to violate my trust. You do understand?"

"Of course, yes. Certainly."

"And this move, our move now, is for my job as well. I can't tell you everything about it, except to say that it's not criminal, that it's something that the good guys do. The protectors do. Do you understand what I mean?"

"So you work for the government then, is that what you're saying?"

He threw his arm around her shoulder and brought her closer to him. "I will explain everything to you in time, all in due time. In the meantime, just trust me. Do you trust me, Emmy?"

She sat up, smiling into his face, her features softening as she studied his eyes, his mouth, his ears. She let her fingers gently comb through his hair and then brush across his lips. "I will do absolutely anything you ask, Adamis. Your secrets are safe with me. I promise that. And I promise that wherever you go I will go. I might ask a bunch of questions but you don't need to give me all those answers. As long as I know that you're working on something good. Does that make sense?"

"It does. And I am."

He showed her the pictures of the warehouse, and the small cottage he also had secured on the beach at Sea Turtle Beach.

"This little place is small, and needs work, but it's on the white sand on the Florida Gulf Coast. It's a very tiny town with a small population, there aren't any huge condo buildings here, and the population is sparse in the summer and fall, but gets overflowing Thanksgiving through May. I've read some studies on the area and I think you'll like it. I think it isn't the Magic Kingdom, but I think you'll like it. About two hours away from your magic place. It's normal, it's not a big city, and the crime rate is very low. I think we can live there without having to worry about our lives being upended again."

She leaned over his lap, examining the pictures he showed on the tablet. "It does look like it needs a lot of work."

"Yes, unfortunately, in the price range I can afford, it has to be that way. But it isn't anything we cannot do, and look at this." He brought up pictures of a huge, old-style tiled bathroom. "You see what I'm seeing?"

"I like all the tile. Looks big!"

"In that corner there, we take out the tub, and what could we put in there?"

"A shower. Your shower!"

"No, Emmy. Our shower."

"Oh, I cannot wait, Adamis. I want to go there to-day!"

"We'll make it so, sweetheart." He nearly choked on his word. He'd never called her that before. She had gone back to looking over the pictures again. Did she notice?

"What about this warehouse? Why do you need a warehouse?"

"That's a fair question. The company does some manufacturing and research, and we need to have a place to set up shop and to do our work. This also is going to need some work, and we'll be creating a small complex here for the workers who come to assist us."

"Will I be able to help you? I want to. I want to be part of it."

It warmed him that she did want to be part of it. But it was too soon, and much too dangerous. Without all his systems in place, it was out of the question, for now.

"In time, but first I have to get it set up, and then we put the personnel in place where I need them, and then slowly we'll incorporate. But don't expect to have a job for the next few months, okay?"

"I'm good with that. As long as we're together. As long as we get out of here."

"So, how was your day? We haven't talked about that at all."

He saw worry lines cross her forehead.

"Emmy? What's up?"

"There was a huge fight downstairs; I saw it from the window. I did like you said and didn't go out on the balcony, but I could see from the window it was two groups of ruffians or gang members fighting each other, and someone was hurt. The security forces came, not the local police. They whisked him away, and the rest of the groups scattered into the streets and disappeared. A few minutes later, someone else came along and hosed off the sidewalk. There was a lot of blood spilled. I'm sure the fellow was killed."

"I'm sorry you had to see that. Glad you remained inside. Now you see why I don't want you going out on your own."

"Yes, I do now. It made me nervous. I hate fights. And now that I recall, the security at the house where I worked was very, very tight. And they were starting to see people coming in causing incidents. There were whispers about girls getting abused by strangers, so security had to be beefed up. I'm just noticing this happening more and more all over. Like some cancer is spreading. It bothers me. I hope we are able to get out and get out quickly."

"Well, the good news is, we have a place to go. But you mustn't tell anyone. And the good news is I think we don't have to wait to sell this property, so we may just leave and do it later. So, tomorrow I would like us to begin packing. We'll get some travel clothes for you, and I'll apologize in advance for buying things that you will hate wearing, but I need to get you a few things so we can leave. And then we'll take off probably within a week. Maybe sooner. I want to be ready by tomorrow, midday. If we have to leave quickly, I want to be able to."

"Why the urgency? Is there some artificial time limit here?"

"Yes, and no." Adamis had to be careful not to reveal anything about Darius. "I am depending on others, and, depending on what they're able to achieve affects when we leave. But, when we go, Emmy, we will never return again. Remember when I asked you if there was anyone you couldn't bear to be separated from? Is that still the case? Think about never coming back. Does anyone come to mind?"

"Everybody I cared about is either dead or gone. I'm ready. You're the one who's not ready Adamis! You have a lot more things to pack than I do. I've just got a nightie, one set of underwear, some baggy pants and a couple of wrinkled shirts." She smiled. "And I have you."

He held her against him. Tight. "Yes, you do, don't you?" They kissed, and then she invited him into the shower. He promised he would join her and, while she trotted off, he sent his message to Darius.

"I've initiated all the purchases, and made contact with everyone I need to. I'm glad you set something up for Cherry because I would not have had the time. But we are ready, will be packed and ready to leave at noon tomorrow. I have accomplices, people I think I can trust. Let me know how your tests go. I await your response, your son."

The answer came back quickly.

*'Thank you for this, my son. I will fall asleep now, warmed with the knowledge that we've put into place everything we can so that you can carry out your prime directive, to protect humans, to make the world a better place. I trust that you will follow that path unwaveringly, and that you will allow others to follow you as well. I go to my resting place probably tomorrow. I have put in the paperwork stating that your departing should be complete by tomorrow night. I have set up*

the parts that need to be turned in, and I have altered some dates on several of them so that they will jive with your recent updates. Godspeed, my son, don't be afraid, be of good courage. Remember who you are and what you are and why you were made. Your father.'

# CHAPTER 15

E MMY HELPED ADAMIS pack many of his clothes, several books that he had stored and used over the years, including some of his favorites, *Gulliver's Travels*, *1001 Arabian Nights*, and a *Holy Bible*. He had some mementos that he had gathered, pictures of him and his maker, and small items from his kitchen that he loved using, such as the lemon peeler and his potato slicer. He was in love with French fries, whether they were potatoes or sweet potatoes.

*AIs fall in love with inanimate objects easily. I once knew one who became obsessed with trains. It nearly cost him and his maker their lives,* Darius had told him once.

Emmy seemed to take great delight at looking at all his personal things, examining them one by one.

"You have no pictures of your family here. Where are they?"

Adamis stood, holding an arm full of T-shirts,

pausing to give her a respectable answer. He had never thought to explain this before, but, of course, it made sense, that she would ask. He should have thought of it. Of course, it had to be a story, since he wasn't allowed to really tell her the truth.

"Much to my sadness, there was a house fire, and everything that was my childhood was destroyed in it. I thought perhaps things would start to show up, through other family or friends, but they never did. I lost everything when I lost my parents."

"Your parents died in the fire? How awful."

Now he was stuck. He felt like a butterfly not yet dead, pinned to its grave in a butterfly collection case. Adamis wasn't sure he should continue with this type of lie, but he'd already committed himself to it and so decided the best rule would be to make light of it, shorten it, and take her inquiry and completely shut it down.

"It happened before I came here, and, unfortunately, it's still painful for me to think about or talk about. Do you mind if maybe we do this later when we aren't so stressed and trying to get our things gathered?"

"Of course, Adamis. I'm sorry I upset you. I just never knew about your family, and I was hoping amongst your things you would have something that pictured you with them. You have pictures of your boss, but not them."

His anger flared a bit, so he adjusted his sensors. "So now you understand, correct?" He sent a directive her way, testing to see if he could actually alter her own brain patterns. He wasn't sure it was working until he finally saw her eyes glaze over for a second and then adopt a completely different attitude.

"So what do you want me to pick up next?" she asked.

She appeared to have completely lost the train of thought. He was disappointed with himself for having learned this, but judged it was important. He would pay for it later, he knew. But, in the interests of time and to further the goal, he justified it.

And then he thought better of it.

*'Remember who you are and why you were made.'*

That did it. The voice clip in his head reminded him of his core value. This lie could be harmful, and it wasn't honorable.

"Emmy, I'm sorry, I wasn't exactly truthful. I was adopted, and I do not remember anything of my parents. It was told to me that they were lost, and I'm sorry, but I never had any pictures. I never remembered them, due to the trauma I may have suffered. All memory of my growing up is gone. I've tried, but there is no fixing that. My adoptive father let me know that they were no longer alive, so it was pointless to try to find them. I told you it was difficult, because nobody wants to hear that they have no parents. I did, I just never knew them."

He watched for her reaction.

"I'm sorry. I didn't mean to pry. As long as you've made your peace with it. I didn't mean to cause you any pain."

"Maybe we can explore this later, after we get re-settled."

"Maybe your adoptive father could help. And, by the way, have you told him?"

"I have. And I'm sure he will." He sensed she was accepting the story, which was partially true, but not in the sense she had grabbed it.

And then she added, "I want to meet that man."

"Yes, in time, anything is possible."

Hoping that would be the end of it for now, he set the shirts down in the suitcase and added a few more items from the bathroom, including his favorite cologne, his favorite brush, a towel and his favorite soap, Number VI, created and blended for the first president of his country, called in that day the United States of America, Mr. Washington. Adamis had learned quite a bit about George Washington, and knew that there was a sometimes contentious relationship between Washington and his DNA ancestor, Thomas Jefferson. It gave him great pride to wear George Washington's cologne and use his soap.

"So are we nearly ready?" he asked.

"Yes, I finished your books and some papers. Are you taking your printer, because I have room?"

"Yes. Good idea! Let's take it so that we can reproduce things that we find along the way."

He explained that he wanted to leave some things behind in case their travel was investigated, and it would appear they were coming back. He put the suitcases by the door, one for Adamis and the other one for Emmy that really was for Adamis as well.

"I have a little bit of time to see if I can pick up some clothes for you, do you want me to do that?"

She swooned and quickly maneuvered into his arms, whispering, "I think we could spend our time doing something else first. We can always buy clothes for me on the way."

"I could be persuaded, you know."

"Are we flying or are we driving, I forgot to ask!"

"I have arranged a flight."

"More surprises. I love them. When does it take off?"

"It's a corporate jet, so when I call them they will be ready within the hour. Have you ever been in a corporate jet?"

"Never. Is it different? I suppose it is, since billionaires and public officials ride in them all the time, don't they?"

"Yes, they do." He stood close to her, so close he could feel the temperature of her skin rising, and hear the ragged breathing deep inside her chest. He placed his arms around her waist and pulled her tight against him. "There are lots of special things on board, and I'm sure you're going to enjoy them all. We'll have about four hours, five hours to kill."

"A bed?"

"A vibrating bed."

She giggled and he loved the feeling of her body against him when she was happy.

"And they have beverages and nice food?"

"I made sure that there were tamales. Probably more than you can eat."

"Perfect."

Adamis was interrupted by an urgent signal, a text message on his AI scanner from the Security Chicks. "I have to take this."

Emmy took a seat in the living room and waited for him.

"They have moved a large ship next to us, twice our size, and configured with weaponry, which is batshit crazy on a prison barge. Appears they have three or four hundred crew. Maybe they're prisoners, but it's mighty strange. We're supposed to be boarded and get a briefing this afternoon. I'm nervous, we all are. How are you coming with things?" Cherry messaged him.

"All arranged. Someone should be reaching out to you, momentarily," He texted back.

"Well, you better fucking hurry, because I think the shit's about to hit the fan."

"I've been delayed, but I will be in touch shortly. I'm doing a project and will be tied up for a few hours, but, on my highest authority, there is someone available to you. And, Cherry, I have a package that will be left for you at the delivery office near my condo. You know it?"

"Yeah, we've used it as well. For me, you say?"

"You need to get away and pick it up. It will be there in just a few. Try to get it first before your meeting."

"You'll be off the grid then for a few?"

"Not sure how long, but I'll be in touch. Not to worry, we got this. There are others."

"God bless you, Adamis. I hope wherever you're going that you are safe."

He next tried to text a note to Darius, but the file was returned unopened. That meant only one thing.

Darius was no longer going to be in the picture.

Next, he texted Cisco on one of the untraceable phones he'd gotten. "I have arranged for someone to help the Security Chicks, but things are moving rapidly and he has not made contact. Do you have the ability to get in touch with her? See if you can help?"

"Absolutely. She have a phone?"

"I'm setting that up now."

"Okay, I'm moving myself."

"What? Moving? Where?"

"Can't say, but they have closed the restaurant. Things are, as you say, happening quickly. I will be in touch shortly, as soon as I can."

"And the Chicks? Will that be a problem?"

"I'll get that done today. So, you're off?"

"I believe so. Have not received that message yet but I think that means we are a go."

"Do it quick, friend. I'm not sure how long any of us will be able to contact one another. The phones will help. I'm erasing all our texts, and you should do the same. Switch to one of your phones and only use that for anything outbound. And don't forget to give out the others."

Adamis put on gloves and handed a pair to Emmy. "Do not touch anything downstairs. Nothing, okay?"

Adamis had planned to stop by the lab and give

Connor one of his cells, but thought better of it and decided to leave a package for him at the delivery office, where he could pick it up later. He wrapped two phones for Cherry in a towel, put it in a mailing box, and wrote her name on the outside. Then he did the same for Connor, giving him three devices. In each box, he gave out his personal number.

Tucking the boxes into one of the bags, he took Emmy's gloved hand and they headed to the door. He took one last glance at his piece of paradise, his refuge, and what he'd always thought was the most secure location he could find. Now it had suddenly turned into feeling like a prison, a trap. But it was still the place where he first learned about sex, where he rescued Emmy, where he dreamed about Darius and all the things they could do together. He was leaving all that behind. Soaking it all in, he steeled himself for the leap, like a tiny young bird learning to fly for the first time.

"I hope I haven't forgotten anything," he whispered to her.

And then he remembered some of the words Darius had said over and over to him over the years of their collaboration, their lifetime together.

*'Remember who you are, why you were made. You're perfect. Now go out there and be perfect.'*

They wheeled the suitcases downstairs and, upon entering the lobby, he heard a commotion brewing, getting louder by the second. Several of the condo's residents were gathered in the corner just off of the street, surrounded by several special security bearing the same uniform as the security guard manning the desk. There was shouting and protests from the group. They had been banned from entering the building to return to their units.

He heard several of them protesting, asking who had given the order to detain them, and there were no answers being given, just references to a state of emergency order that had been placed for the entire building. Adamis tried not to stare and yanked on Emmy's hand when she started gawking at the situation.

"Don't pay attention, please. We have to get out of here," he whispered.

At the security desk, he nodded, and before they crossed fully around the corner, the guard called out to them. Adamis turned slowly, presenting himself full-frontal, kept his jaw stiff and firm, eyed him with his glare and addressed him. Adamis didn't think he'd seen him before.

"I'm sorry, but you have to show your papers."

"To leave the building?"

"It's a new rule, for security. We just received the orders not more than an hour ago. Everyone's being detained, going and coming. Unless they have prior permission."

Adamis knew what he had to do. He pulled out a piece of paper from his jacket pocket, holding it up to the security guard's face. All it was was an authorization to travel, signed by Darius himself, that Adamis had used when he traveled on business elsewhere. With a heavy dose of telepathy, he planted the suggestion in the guard's mind that this was acceptable authorization. He saw the gentleman read the paper with his eyes slightly glazed over, and then nod, addressing them to leave by the front door. One of the guards detaining the group turned and shouted out after Adamis and Emmy as they reached the door.

"He's okay, I saw his papers and his authorization to travel. I checked it out myself."

Reluctantly, the security guard hoisted his semi-automatic back over his shoulder and went back to monitoring and controlling the group in the lobby.

They exited the building, walked several blocks, and then hailed a cab, asking to be delivered to the delivery office address. Adamis didn't want the cab to wait for them, so, after he left the boxes, he hailed another cab to take him to the small private airport next to the bay. He had texted for the plane, but was told when he got there that it was not available yet, and then it had to pass certain last-minute inspections.

This didn't set well with Adamis who knew that something else was afoot. He asked the representative if there was another plane available, something that could take him to New York, since he didn't want to reveal where they were headed. The attendant told him they had a cancellation for this morning, someone who was taking a business trip and had been detained.

"They've already been cleared for a path to New York; however, the other gentleman is not able to travel now. The rates will double, but the pilot and crew are still available if you wish to take it. But you must be quick. They'll be leaving in a few minutes."

"I will take it." He handed the attendant his credits, and, after double checking the verification, the attendant nodded and spoke instructions into a headset, getting the plane ready to take off.

"Mr. Jefferson, it will only take about five, maybe ten minutes. They're already fueled. You have luggage I can take?"

"No, thanks. We'll take them with us."

"Very well, have a seat; we'll call you in just a few."

The private airport was extremely luxurious. Gorgeous pictures of exotic locations hung on the walls. In normal times, this room would probably be filled with billionaires and captains of industry, taking their families or girlfriends on exotic trips to foreign lands. But, even with all the travel posters and eye candy, Adamis had a hard time calming himself down. He didn't want to disconnect any of his systems, because his high alert status needed to remain fully functioning. Otherwise, he might miss something that could be costly.

But Emmy, she was in total panic mode, even shaking.

"It's going to be okay. Remember what I told you?"

"Yes," she said as her teeth chattered, looking out at the runway and watching a sleek jet approach the observation windows and gate area.

Absentmindedly, she whispered, "You said there would be tamales. But I'm not going to hold you to it this time."

Adamis hugged her tightly, and kissed her forehead. "I have one more communication to make before we take off."

He reached inside the briefcase he carried and pulled out his tablet given to him by Darius. He was going to try one more time.

When he turned it on, he knew that the time had arrived. He was notified on the tablet that a duplicate file had been made but that no further communication would be allowed on the old channel. This meant that his maker was probably already gone, or going into surgery. It was the end of one chapter, and the beginning of a whole new one. This was real, this wasn't a fake, and it terrified him.

He put the tablet away in his briefcase, took out his AI channel device, and sent Connor the message about the package left for him at the delivery station. "It's in a mailbox, with your name on it, and they'll hold it there for a week. When you get it, you push the button at the bottom and it will give you the telephone number of the phone. There's only one contact in there and that's my phone. You need to get in touch with me later on. I will not be available until this evening. Take care, godspeed. They are all over us, everywhere. Be safe."

# CHAPTER 16

ADAMIS AND EMMY scrambled up the gangway, getting help from the copilot with their suitcases. They elected to keep the luggage close to them, rather than stowing them in the belly of the jet. Adamis was shown how to operate his electronics using the satellite system located on the plane. He knew this to be a secure connection, although not always reliable in connectivity.

Although still a modern and newer model, the plane was strictly business class, not with the opulence of the one he had reserved earlier. It also was a bit smaller.

"Do you know what happened to the plane that I ordered? What the holdup was?" he asked the crew.

The pilot shook his head. "I've been hearing from several of my friends that there are lots of cancellations going on. I don't quite get it, I mean usually people are able to travel when they say they are, within a few hours, of course. But this is the third one I've heard of today, and we've had cancellations in Chicago and New York as well. Now, I have a flight plan for LaGuardia, is that where you're headed?"

"No, we were unfortunately forced to change our itinerary. I checked with my office and now we're headed to Tampa."

"Very well, I will have to get working on that right now. When we are cleared to go, I will let you know before we take off."

"Will it take time? I was told these things can be changed in a matter of seconds."

He laughed. His copilot assumed his seat in the cockpit while the pilot dallied behind. "That's been a change that took place last month. Nothing is standard, routine, anymore. Nothing is quick. Everything is complicated, overly so, in my opinion. And it's getting worse, I fear."

"I didn't hear about that, but I guess not paying much attention. I don't fly often."

"Surely you've been reading the papers and check-ing the news. I hear it sometimes first there, believe it or not."

"You mean the riots, uprisings?"

He shrugged. "That, and everything else. Nothing makes sense anymore. Surely you must be noticing that."

Adamis was keenly aware of issues with permissions, crowd control and public demonstrations in California, but he had not realized it had already spread to other parts of the country. He made it a choice not to read newspapers or watch television, but he'd seen several reports as he walked the streets of Emery City.

They settled into their adjoining seats, luxuriously upholstered in white leather, the white and light brown coloring seeming to be a theme. There was a full-sized bathroom in the rear, their cabin attendant said, and a bedroom, "However, I understand you ordered a king-sized bed. This is much smaller, but it has a nice mattress, or so I've been told," he added.

About twenty minutes later, a Jeep arrived nearby, carrying four military men on their way to a large jet roughly a quarter mile away. The plane had been heading toward the hangar when it was stopped and boarded by the security personnel with the same grey and blue uniforms. They ran up the stairs and disappeared inside.

"I think that was our jet. And it appears the military wanted to stop it," Adamis whispered to Emmy.

Her eyes were on wide angle, fully alert, afraid. "Are we going to be able to leave? Adamis, I'm scared."

"Try not to be–and I know that's a tall order." He

held out his hand on the padded divider, and she placed hers inside before he folded his fingers over hers.

"Can I serve you a mimosa, or would you prefer something else?" The male attendant asked.

"You want champagne at this time of day?" Adamis asked, as he smiled.

"I don't know what I want. I think what I want most of all is just to take off. I need to get in the sky. I'm scared to death."

The attendant smiled down to her. "I can tell you're not used to flying. No worries, our captain is a former jet pilot. Decorated Air Force veteran. You're in the best hands you could possibly be."

"So is that the jet that we had asked for?" Adamis asked him.

"I'm not sure who that is; I do know that whomever had contracted it also canceled. The crew went home."

"I think maybe Emmy and I should try a mimosa. And once we get into the air, maybe another."

"You got it. Be right back." Quickly returning, he handed each of them a small plate of nuts, dried fruit, and assorted cheeses, and disappeared into the galley.

"You should eat something, Emmy; it will calm your nerves."

"I can't think about eating. What's taking so long?"

"I'm not sure, but they do have to file a flight plan, and normally that's done the morning before or evening before. But they can do it quicker. There must be a shortage somewhere."

The pilot came from the cockpit, sat down on a seat that swiveled around so he could face both of them. "It seems that they are having some kind of situation in the tower. I'm not exactly sure what's the issue, an operational control protocol or something, but I can't get a straight answer. Do you have any knowledge of what's going on here? I mean, are you involved in any of this? Is there something I need to know?"

Adamis thought about this before he spoke. "You mean, are we criminals, a flight risk? Fugitives?"

"I didn't mean to sound harsh, but—"

"Here's what I can tell you, what I do know, and it isn't for certain. I lied about knowing that there are armed insurrections going on everywhere. We were almost not allowed to leave our condo complex. I have friends who have been detained all over San Francisco and Emery City. I understand it's happening in other parts too, but thought it was just California. But let me tell you this, and I am not going to admit that I said it to you. I believe we are in the midst of a revolution, being perpetrated by people we don't need to trust. I can pay you double your salary if you will get this plane up in the air in the next ten minutes. Because, frankly, none of us are going to be able to leave this airport if you don't."

"And you have knowledge of this because?"

Emmy barged in, urgency lacing her words. "He works for the government. He's a protector. That's what he does is keep people safe. Now you should listen to him and get this plane off the ground right now. We're all in grave danger. You don't want to hesitate. You have to act now. Right now."

The pilot looked at his hands folded on his lap. "I was beginning to feel like the old days when I used to fly jets and do bombing runs, that it was almost getting to be that bad. But now, forces invading our cities, banding up innocent people? I'm not so sure I sit well with what I've been told by my colleagues. Let me do what you ask, but I want some answers once we get in the air. Agreed?"

"You bet. Let's get going."

Adamis could hear some of the chatter going on over his headsets once he returned to his seat. The control tower was balking at giving clearance. The pilot maintained a cool demeanor, claimed he was having issues with his headset, his copilot tried to cut in but it sounded like they were having electrical issues. And

Adamis knew they were probably faking it. In less than five minutes, the engines were fully revved up and they were taxiing down the runway. Adamis heard squawking and shouting coming over the headsets that the pilot and copilot were wearing, but both gentlemen shook their heads, stuck to their instruments, and lifted off the ground. It wasn't until they were airborne that Adamis saw there was a convoy of Jeeps and trucks headed for them, but, miraculously, were too late to stop the jet.

The two travelers sat back and sipped on their mimosas while Adamis continued to monitor what the pilot was hearing. He also understood several other private pilots were making pleas, asking for information, like there had been some kind of a private circuit that emerged, and Adamis learned that other pilots were having the same problems, some of them having their entire crew, and passengers, taken away, luggage seized, and two pilots were reportedly arrested.

It didn't take long before they crossed the California border into Nevada, and then arced down headed for Texas.

Adamis pulled out his tablet and checked the data that had been copied and resubmitted to his hard drive, under security codes he had used before with Darius. He was relieved to find all the material was accessible still. No messages had been received, so he assumed that this part of the mission was over.

He replaced his tablet with his AI device, and attempted to leave a message for Cisco, which apparently did not go through. He tried contacting the Security Chicks, and they too were inaccessible. Then he tried contacting Connor, and found the same. He quickly closed the device, and sat back sipping on his mimosa again. In assessing what was going on, he didn't want to reveal what the phone numbers were for the devices he'd been given, so would wait until they landed before doing so.

Nearly an hour later, the pilot came back to greet him again.

"Well it appears we've stirred up a hornet's nest. I was informed on my secure line that I share with my former air force buddies that I might have jeopardized my pilot's license. That doesn't make me very happy. So better have some answers for me. And quick."

"I think it was the luck of the draw. This wasn't directed toward you, maybe not even the two of us. It's who you were taking today, the fact that I was here and basically you can tell them I commandeered your plane by force. In a way, that's true."

"Well, that's if I get the chance to tell my side of the story. I may have created such a stir that they will threaten to shoot us down."

"No, we aren't going over any nuclear sites or the White House."

"Oh, great. So that's all you've got? I just ended my career for you. I want some answers."

"I get it. I really do. But, I don't think you had much of a future there anyway, and I don't think you made a mistake, in fact I think you took a big step toward preserving you and your family's safety."

"Well thank God the wife and kids are back east. I told them not to come home. I couldn't explain, and my wife was rather upset."

"As she should be. As we all are. We'll sort it out. But there is something going on in California for sure. And it will settle down eventually, but you don't want to be caught in the crossfire."

"Absolutely not. So what exactly *do* you do?"

"Like Emmy said, I'm a protector. I work for the Adam Project, in San Francisco. We do all kinds of AI work, assess human potential and work on systems to automate some things, improve others. I have worked for years with a team of researchers, some of the best scientists on the planet, and one product developer. Unfortunately, I think that lab has been shut down."

"Why? That's what I don't get."

"It's just a theory. Nothing definite yet, but we're

working on it."

"So what is your official capacity then?"

Adamis was not going to tell him all the truth, at least the truth about his origin. "There are some in my community who believe there is a coup or a takeover happening, at least on the West Coast. And if it spreads to the East Coast, well, we have a problem. Now, I am exploring the possibility of setting up an operation in Florida. Which is why it was so urgent for us to leave. My company has given me funding to do this. If you would like, I might be able to offer you a position if you feel you are able to do so."

"You mean as a pilot?"

"More than that. A negotiator, a communicator to other pilots. To be the point of contact. If this is happening to you today and several of your friends, just imagine what's happening all over the West Coast."

"I suppose we'll find out when we land, won't we?"

"Well, they do know that we're landing in Tampa. That could be a problem."

"So perhaps we should change that trajectory, perhaps we should land in Miami or someplace in the Eastern Seaboard."

"And I could always travel on my own down to Florida. Where are your wife and children?"

"Oddly enough, they're in Boston."

"Then why don't you put a plan ahead to land in Boston. That way if they show up in Tampa expecting to catch you and the plane, they won't find you. And Emmy and I will be long gone."

"Is this safe?"

"You're asking me something I have no capacity to find out. But you'll be with your wife and kids. There are people who have studied what's going on and alerted me to this several months ago, although I didn't pick it up. It's only been within the last week that action plans were put into place and urgently I was helped to get myself and part of the company's assets out of the area. But you are welcome, if you are a patriot, to join our team. I don't know what that will look like, but it's better than waiting to be victimized, to be picked up and disappeared."

"I'm going to consider it. Is this something my co-pilot would be involved with as well?"

"How well do you know him?"

"Not well at all. I think he's a good man, I know Gerald here, my staff, much better. We've worked together for over ten years. He's solid."

"Then I suggest you not work with anybody you're not 100% sure of. Just tell your copilot that we are taking a detour to Boston instead, that there seems to be some kind of ground trouble in Tampa, and let him know that Emmy has received word that she has a sick relative she needs to visit? Something like that. Would that work?"

"Yes, I think so. And then what about the plane?"

"Well, it's not your plane, is it?"

"No, it belongs to the service."

"Then you and your co-pilot can be on your way. Later on, we can touch base and perhaps arrange for you to fly back to Tampa. Or Miami or wherever you feel it's safe. I'll let you arrange that. And ask your attendant if he's interested in joining us."

"So just what do you have in mind? Surely not an armed insurrection?"

"No, not an armed insurrection. What we're trying to do is stop one from occurring, and holding the entire country, perhaps eventually the whole world, hostage. I have humans as well as AI assets that we can deploy and use. I'm just trying to collect honest men and women who don't want to relinquish all their rights and freedoms. I want freedom-loving individuals, who will fight to stay that way."

# CHAPTER 17

T HE MINUTES ADAMIS and Emmy spent above the clouds, free from all the noise of the world below, the quiet hum of the engines, and the very faint elevator music used to calm the rich and famous, the hardworking people of means, and their friends, girlfriends, or families, were special. Sandwiched between all the stress down below and the stress and unexpected challenges that lay ahead, it was truly the quiet before the storm.

Their attendant was good as his word, and brought them multiple glasses of champagne. Emmy fed him grapes. She fed him cheeses. She took huge sips of the wonderful drink and slurped some back to him in private kisses, inviting his hands, distracting his thoughts. In those precious minutes, Adamis saw himself as a human man, a human man in love.

He knew nothing lasted forever. He was aware that not everything that appeared one way actually was that way in reality. People change. People fade and disappear. People disappoint. He vowed never to be any of those. But, yes, he was a person. As perfect as he could be. And he had the capacity to be even greater. It was just as Darius had told him: he would be a leader, relish it, feel the courage of doing something good, really good, at a time when the world needed it.

What was odd for him was that the world wouldn't know who or what he was, at least most of them. His AI buddies would, but they would go to the de-parting conveyor belt rather than betray him. He was sure of that. His hope was that by the time Emmy learned the truth, she wouldn't care.

He saw it now, his premonition. Walking down the beach together, the wind in their faces, her hair blowing in the breeze. The sky was bright orange and purple with enormous clouds that put exclamation points to the sunset, until everyone went home, the birds quieted unless they were going to fish by moonlight. The golf carts would go home. The children were put to bed. Lovers might stay awhile and sneak a few silvery rays of moonlight to add to their kissing, like he and Emmy would do. They were hopelessly in love and inseparable, and together they made a force even greater than his alone. Emmy was the exception to the cautionary tale everyone told him.

"Don't trust humans, and especially human females," Connor had told him.

He thought about that comment as she led him back to the bedroom. He had mimosa splashed on his shirt, and some of it had dripped on his pants. Her dress they'd picked up on the way to the airport was unbuttoned, showing off her shiny cleavage, dripping with the wonderful mixture he would lovingly lick off her skin. He would lose himself in her arms, tune out everything of the cares of the world and their chances for a happily ever after in her moans.

Her eyes were blazing as he followed her into the bedroom. He was going to make her shatter and beg to be taken again. He'd set a new record. All of this made him smile. He told his friend to go fuck off.

*Connor, my friend, I'm sorry, but you are wrong. Wish you had what I'm seeing now.*

She shed her dress over her head. Left with her red bra and very skimpy panties, her hard body, even with the orange juice and champagne stains, was beautiful enough to be mounted in a museum of beautiful women. She was human, and she adored him. That was all he wanted, all he'd perhaps ever wanted, and it was real. He was becoming a real man. He was like Pinocchio who became a real boy, blessed by the fairy godmother. He had a family, a father who loved him, but, most of all, he celebrated that he was real.

And Adamis was becoming real.

Emmy's fingers unzipped his pants, sliding them down over his hips. She unbuttoned his shirt so slowly, he was tempted to ask her to rip it off and ravage him. She would like that, but not tonight. Instead, he was patient. Breathing in and out, filling her head with dreams, planting in her thoughts how wonderful she was going to feel, that each thrust would take her to Heaven and back.

*Can you feel it, Emmy, my love for you? Can you feel how precious you are to me?*

She had dropped to her knees after shedding his boxers, and moaned as she took him in her mouth, nodding her head.

"Tell me more …" she said between sucks.

She thought he'd said those words. How perfect.

*Tell me what you want me to do to you tonight. I want to give you all the pleasure. We have nearly three hours. Tell me how you want it to be ….*

She stood in front of his naked body. Her breasts were still constrained by that red bra. He reached to remove the clasp at the back and she wiggled out of his grip. She shed her panties and walked on all fours on the bed, settling down into the silken pillow and exposed her rear to him. She had a world class butt, not that Adamis was an expert, but he'd never seen flesh so beautiful, so thrilling, so supple and so full of pheromones in every pore.

She laced up and down her slit with her forefinger and then plunged it in to her opening.

That little demonstration nearly had him burst all over her. He climbed up to spoon against her fine ass, his knees just inside hers, his back gently pressing against her back, his fingers finding hers, fondling them and then inserting both hers and his into her opening.

*'I am so glad it was you who took my virginity, Emmy. I never want to ever be with anyone else.'*

It surprised him when he felt her thought come back to him, filled with passion and magic.

*'My pleasure. I love you, Adamis. Make us one. I want to fly out of this plane with you, somewhere no one can find us ever.'*

He inserted himself, then when he was fully seated and very deep, rose up, taking her with him, lifting her perfect ass over his member. He was hard and strong, gently stretching out her arms to above her head, snatching the pillow from the bed and placing it under her soft belly, raising her derriere up sweetly, and then plunging in over and over again with all the force he could muster up until the point of pain, and not yet crossing that threshold, letting up to give her a chance to breathe so he could do it again.

Neither of them spoke for nearly two hours as first he did what she wanted, and then he asked the same of her. They lay facing each other, just gazing, and then the love play would start all over again.

He brought her his glass of bubbly and she drank from him. He picked her up and took her in the shower, while he massaged her hair in the scented shampoo they'd brought. Every touch was an exploration, every kiss a reason to moan, to go higher, to dream a little bigger. He felt them all, her beautiful dreams of the Magic Kingdom when the world was perfect. He showed her his dreams for their future, the little house, the beach, the sunsets, the cheering crowds of people now free and able to live without unfair boundaries, free to choose, to love, to love each other, to be kind, and …

To be better humans.

THE TAP ON the door awakened them. Adamis was getting used to sleeping with her tucked against his chest, so it startled him.

He covered her, slipped on his boxers, and answered the door.

"We are making our descent into Logan Airport. We'll be landing in about ten minutes," the attendant said.

"Thank you."

"May I take your glasses?"

He handed them over and thanked him.

"Would you like anything before we land? I have just a couple of minutes."

"Tiny bit of mineral water and some lime, if you have it. We'll be right out," he whispered.

"Very well, it will be waiting for you. I'll have to strap in in just a few minutes. You'll need to do the same."

"Understood."

He gently woke her up. Her hair was still wet. She didn't want to get up.

"We are landing, sweetheart. Time to get ready for the next leg of the journey."

Emmy bolted up, quickly dressed and tied her wild and still wet hair in a clip. They sat together and enjoyed their refreshing mineral water as they descended through the clouds, the city and Atlantic Ocean in the foreground.

In several minutes, they landed. He pushed out this message to the one who wasn't there.

*'Father, I have made it out of California and we have landed on the east coast. Wish you could tell me what's in store for us next. Whatever it is, I know you will be there with me, with us both.'*

# CHAPTER 18

T HE LANDING IN a private commercial airport in Boston was uneventful. After they taxied over toward the private hangars, the pilots shut off the engines for now, and John Hanson, the pilot, came back to speak to Adamis.

He had anticipated some of the pilot's questions. He handed Hanson one of his phones, which left him with only two remaining, and one of those had to go to Emmy.

"This is how we might communicate. There is only one person in the contact list, and that's the number to the phone I carry. I have other ways of communicating with other people in different circles but this is an untraceable private old school system that can keep us from being detected."

Hanson looked at the pink and turquoise plastic cover around the phone. "Your choice for me? My daughter will be most impressed with your taste."

"Which is why you shouldn't show her. I mean that, John."

Hanson nodded.

Since Emmy was interested in the transaction, he answered her without her question being spoken. "I have one for you as well, sweetheart. We'll go over all that in a bit."

Then he set his attention on the pilot. "So we're going to take a car and drive down to Florida from here, we'll leave right away. If you can, I would like you to stow the plane, use whatever pretense you wish. Then go back to your family in Boston. And await my message. Watch, perhaps find five other pilots or people who can help us with our cause, and ask them each to find five more, John. We're looking for patriots, people who desire to be free."

"I certainly can do that."

"I also want to make sure that the men or women you choose are 100% trustworthy, like people you would have your family stay with in an emergency. We can't convince anybody–we can't insist–and, if they don't willingly come when you make a subtle suggestion about what may be lying ahead for all of us, I don't want you to pursue it. If someone needs to be convinced, they aren't our people. Do you understand?"

"I do. Do you have sufficient financial backing?"

"Well, I do. However, I have no means of replenishing it, so I have to be careful and use it wisely. I'm hoping that most of what we can do is through volunteers. I have a team of researchers and scientists I think I can rely on, and I have other colleagues I've worked with for the past three and a half years, who feel like I do and would go to their grave rather than see any harm come to me or our little movement."

"So are these people officials of some kind or owners of companies?"

"The answer to that is no. I'm not sure we can trust any of those people. I'm not willing to try. These are only scientists and researchers and helpers I've had personal knowledge of and worked and discussed our situation with. It's been organized very briefly–and very quickly–so we have to keep it tight and small; there will be time to expand it later if our first few steps take off. If not, at least we tried. It's a dangerous world out there, John, and it's not getting any safer, and it won't get safer unless we do something."

"I agree completely. So I go to my wife's parents then and probably say nothing to my co-pilot."

"That's correct. Only share what we're doing with those you are absolutely 100% sure will be committed and will not betray us. All we need is one to betray us and it's over. It's very fragile, but, like anything worth doing, if it is a good idea and if it is meant to be, in the old days they would've said, if the Gods are with us, it will work. But we have to keep off the grid, we have to stay out of all the normal forms of communication, and we have to be diligent and patient."

"Thank you for trusting me, Adamis. I promise I won't let you down. I suppose I'm not to say anything to my wife and children?"

"Tell them what you like, but, yes, keep our movement quiet. You can let them know that you've been furloughed, or temporarily let go, that there's so much turmoil in California you think it's wiser for everyone to stay in Boston until all the violence is settled. That could take a while."

"By the way, do you understand that San Francisco is completely under fire?"

"I'm not surprised, John. So how bad is it?"

"Well, from the reports I was able to gather as we were landing, it's worse than the 1906 earthquake and fire. Most of downtown, the Financial District, much of it in flames; rioters and looters have completely sacked the Marina area, trashed City Hall. There's a large encampment of police and security forces taking up base in Golden Gate Park, but they're severely outnumbered, and right now there's a large population of protestors completely surrounding the park, ready to move in and take over. The report I saw is that there's going to be a wholesale mass massacre of these security forces. I'm afraid for the consequences of that."

"Good idea to get out of the Bay Area then. I feel for all the people on the peninsula, all the owners of companies who have supported and made that such a vibrant research and development area. No doubt they'll be fleeing as fast as they can, and I do think they'll be fleeing whether or not they have permission. I'm sure whoever it was who had commandeered the other plane wishes he'd been able to get out."

"Several of my pilots have been arrested and no one's heard anything further. I am truly scared for what's going on."

"I think, John, you have to understand, that this is orchestrated by just probably a handful of people who are seeking to overthrow everything that this country worked for for hundreds of years. And they have their sights set on the world next. I think our founding forefathers, and I am related–at least distantly related–to Thomas Jefferson's family, I'm sure that if the Founding Fathers knew what was going on, they would stand and fight. I don't think they would allow it to be. They paid a high price for their freedom, and now it's not even being subtly taken away; it's being snatched from the hands and fists of babies and mothers and grandmothers and men who refuse to stand. I don't want to fight them, John, I want to beat them. I want to be smarter than them. I want to work harder, with a more committed cadre of like-minded people. There are more of us than there are of them. Just remember that."

"How fortunate we were that this plane had been canceled. I can't thank you enough, Adamis."

"Thank me when it's done, John. And pray to God we all survive."

Emmy peppered Adamis with questions until the taxi arrived to take them to a car lot so they could purchase a van or suburban-type vehicle for the long trip down to Florida. After they'd made their purchase and were heading out, she finally was able to ask him, "So what does this mean for us? I mean, are we just going to stay in a little house at the beach? It seems like we need to go to some kind of military base or a fort somewhere. Aren't people going to be looking for us?"

"Not yet. I don't think they'll put it together yet. Like I said, we have to be smarter. But nothing would please me more than to just be on a permanent vacation. But how long is that going to be, I don't know. When will they find everybody who's doing that and round them up and take control of that too? I honestly do think they want to control every aspect of our lives.

Nobody has thought of this. Did you even consider it when you were growing up, when you were working at the house, when you thought your biggest problems were trying to avoid the fists and slaps and punches of your handler?"

Adamis felt the little slip. He had called Emmy's boss her handler, but it did seem to fit. She had been no more free to be herself than Adamis had been as he was developing, being created, and what the rules and the environment were when he came to being. They were like two sides of the same coin.

"Did you know about this all along?" she asked.

"Not really. I mean, my father knew about it a little bit, knew more than he told me. But when he began to reveal certain things to me and, well he helped me with the purchases, and he did that by leaving me assets and money, and a team. My understanding is that probably his old company will be shut down permanently, as will everything else I was involved in. So the money he gave me will enable me to start up again and perhaps recreate some of the magic that we did. I think I can do it."

Emmy hesitated, then held his hand in her left as he drove, "I know you can, Adamis."

They switched sides and Adamis adopted the passenger side so he could get up to date with his communications. One of the items that he had brought in the suitcase was a portable electronic cell system, independent of any other system, easily installed in the ceiling of the van. He used it to access some of the traditional news media outlets and saw the pictures of San Francisco. Also, he saw the pictures of the large prison ship anchored next to the Security Chicks' much smaller ship in the Bay.

There wasn't much said about it except the flashing of the two ships side by side as the pictures panned in on Oakland and the Oakland Hills, also fully engulfed in flames. That meant perhaps the city of Emery was also gone, which would mean all those security forces had either moved on elsewhere, been hired up or had been eliminated. He hoped to God that the Chicks got the help they needed in order to stabilize, but in examining the pictures, he did not see evidence of anyone on either ship. And that alarmed him.

He arranged communication with Connor and with Cisco. Cisco had done what he'd asked and hired his group to move the warehouse contents, including all the specialized chemicals that needed to be refrigerated, with climate controlled trucks that were already on their way to leaving the California territory. Cisco had a team of ten, and they each were divided amongst the trucks: one for driving, switching over driving, and the rest for security. They were given the address of the new warehouse in Florida and were not planning to stop along the way except for fuel.

That was something that worried Adamis, that they had to still buy fuel, so he wondered if there would be a way they could convert these trucks and any kind of vehicles they needed to all electric since using them would be untraceable–as long as the vehicles' computer systems were adapted for their communication only. He made that a note to take care of as soon as he got set up.

They passed through several states on their way down, headed through North and South Carolina, Georgia, and soon crossed the Florida line, which gave him a huge sigh of relief.

Connor contacted him to let him know that he and a group of six researchers and scientists had dismantled the lab as best they could, taken key components they would need, and were also on their way to Florida to meet them at the warehouse. Connor said that Leon had been arrested, and they didn't want to wait to try to fight to get him back.

"We'll have to do that later, Connor, but right now I have no plans to go back to California for a while, at least until we're set up. Do you have any way of reaching him or getting word to him?"

Connor answered, "Not reliably. I'm sorry about this. But perhaps it's for the best. We are getting ready to leave as soon as it's dark; we've lost several members of the old research team, not people I contacted, and the group I'm taking is extremely committed and totally freaked out. We're going to get there as fast as we can, and I've got a really jittery and nervous bunch of humans and AIs that are almost blowing their circuits as well as their gaskets, their human gaskets that is."

Adamis answered him with a smiley face. "Thank you for your loyalty and your trust in me, Connor. I do believe we're going to make this work. And if not, well?"

Connor answered back, "Oh, hell, I think I was always programmed for a good fight. Somewhere in my own DNA there must have been a shit disturber. I'm living my own dream, Adamis. And it had to happen, Adamis. Only a matter of time. I refuse to sit back and allow myself to be passively de-parted. They don't even give us a funeral."

"Why should they? We don't go to Heaven. No one grieves over our bodies when we're gone."

"Not so. Some of us will be missed. There has to be some big computer in the sky we sail off to, get zapped, surrounded with sex bots to spend eternity with."

"Maybe you'll have the time some day to write the first AI novel all about it."

"I hear that's already been done."

"No, written by an AI. Story by an AI, not directed by a human. It could happen, you know."

"My handler is still alive, and he would put me down so quickly if someone pressed his buttons hard enough. God love him, for giving me my existence, but I have to do this."

"Did you disable your connection?"

Adamis had instructed all of the AI members of his community how to do so. Just as a fail-safe in case the worst happened. Little did he know at the time that it was going to happen.

"It was the first thing I did. He's probably stewing over the fact he can't reach me but doesn't want to come out of that cave he lives in. He lives in So. San Francisco, you know. And I'm not staying in the warehouse. So it's adios, California, and adios to all this shit."

"Oh, and, by the way, what about the Security Chicks? Where are they?"

"I heard it from another AI, not one of us, that they got what was coming to them. Some guy pulled up in a big old truck and hauled them all away. He said, 'They're headed for the bottom of the Grand Canyon.'"

"Excellent."

"Huh? You got to be kidding."

"I don't think that's what really happened. I think Darius' guy got them out. It's the only way it could have happened and been allowed to happen. I didn't see any persons on the ship when I looked at pictures when we landed. What's going on with that?"

"I don't think anybody cares. Have you seen what's happened to Oakland and the hills?"

"Yes, I have. So that's where everybody's focus is?"

"If ever there was a time to smuggle out almost fifty bitchy, highly tactical and independent female AIs, that was the time. I think you're right, Adamis. They got out."

He made several other communications and referenced some bank accounts to transfer funds to new places in Florida he had set up in advance. He needed to have credits, he needed to have liquid cash, and he needed to purchase items and complete the transactions he'd already set up. He had the local representatives to meet with and consummate the deals, and he could do that as soon as they arrived. He didn't want to wait any longer to close them than he had to.

They pulled into the Tampa area around noon the next day, Adamis driving, Emmy was trying to sleep in the back and having difficulty. But Adamis had no problem staying awake as long as he didn't have to concentrate on making communications elsewhere. Seeing the water and the boats in the Tampa Bay area brightened his spirit. He'd seen pictures, but had never been to this part of the country before.

Crossing the bridge to the barrier outer islands, he stumbled upon the Belleair Beach sign and followed the GPS directions to the house.

"Emmy, Emmy, look. We're here. It's not pretty, and it's not perfect, but it's home."

She sleepily woke up and took her position next to him on the passenger side. "Oh my god, it's beautiful, Adamis. Look at that beach. It's like sugar."

"It's the sweetest thing I've ever seen. This really feels like home, doesn't it?"

"Can we get out?"

"You bet! In just a couple of days, this is going to be ours, so absolutely. I don't have any keys, but I know I can figure out a way to get in."

"I don't care what the house looks like. Look at that water and the sand and look at the sky and look at the birds. There are no fires, no people, no signs. There are no sirens or police cars. It's just this little shack, the white sugar sand beach, the big blue sky. And look at those clouds!"

Adamis knew it was going to work. He was starting to see premonitions of the life of their future. He got out of the van, took her hand, and they walked around the house to the sand. They walked up and down first to the left and then to the right, passing a handful of people on their way. It was a weekday so there were no crowds, no children sitting there playing in the sand, as everyone was either working or back in school. But an old fisherman sat on a creaky, rusty chair fishing into the waves.

As they walked past, Adamis looked at the pail and saw it was only filled with bait, he hadn't caught anything yet.

"Best of luck, sir, hope you catch a bunch," Adamis said.

"Oh, I will, I put my fishing line into the water, and they come. I've just begun. We're going to be very lucky today. And thanks," the old man said to his back.

Adamis stopped, turned to study him, and almost could see the face of his maker, of his father, of Darius.

He walked back toward the gentleman. "Darius?"

"Did you really think I'd leave you, son?"

Thank you for reading Free to Love: Free As A Bird.

I hope that you will share this series with others and that you will leave me a review.

I have designed the Free To Love series into five main chapters, books in the series:

Free As A Bird                     Romance

Science Of The Heart

The Promise Directive

New Beginnings

You can view them all here when they become available the end of this year and into next year. All 5 with the promise of love everlasting and a community

and family of heroes, AI and human, creating a magical
world in the likeness and imagination of a father,
and son.

Hope you will continue the journey!

Other books by S. Hamil here.
authorsharonhamilton.com/meet-s-hamil

## ABOUT THE AUTHOR

 Author S. Hamil is the dark side pen name and twisted sister for author Sharon Hamilton. She indulges her creative juices to bring you tales of love, love lost, adventure and redemption in a good vs. evil power struggle between all her paranormal and fantasy worlds ruled by good and evil characters. Her NYT and USA/Today Golden Vampires of Tuscany and Guardians Series paint colorful tales where True Love Heals all wounds in the Gardens of the Heart. These angels, dark angels and Golden Vampires, as well as the humans who are caught in their web follow a bumpy path to redemption with stories you'll stay up all night reading and crave for more. Definitely not what they taught you in Sunday School.

She loves hearing from her fans:
Sharonhamilton2001@gmail.com

Her website is:

sharonhamiltonauthor.com

Find out more about S. Hamil, her upcoming releases, appearances and news when you sign up for S. Hamil's newsletter.

Facebook:

facebook.com/SharonHamiltonAuthor

Twitter:

twitter.com/sharonlhamilton

Pinterest:

pinterest.com/AuthorSharonH

Amazon:

amazon.com/Sharon-Hamilton/e/B004FQQMAC

BookBub:

bookbub.com/authors/sharon-hamilton

Youtube:

youtube.com/channel/UCDInkxXFpXp_4Vnq08ZxM BQ

Soundcloud:

soundcloud.com/sharon-hamilton-1

S. Hamil's Rockin' Romance Readers:

facebook.com/groups/sealteamromance

S. Hamil's Goodreads Group:
goodreads.com/group/show/199125-sharon-hamilton-readers-group

Visit S. Hamil's Online Store:
sharon-hamilton-author.myshopify.com

Join S. Hamil's Review Teams:

eBook Reviews:
sharonhamiltonassistant@gmail.com

Audio Reviews:
sharonhamiltonassistant@gmail.com

**Life** *is one fool thing after another.*
**Love** *is two fool things after each other.*

# REVIEWS

## PRAISE FOR THE
## GOLDEN VAMPIRES OF TUSCANY SERIES

"Well to say the least I was thoroughly surprise. I have read many Vampire books, from Ann Rice to Kym Grosso and few other Authors, so yes I do like Vampires, not the super scary ones from the old days, but the new ones are far more interesting far more human than one can remember. I found Honeymoon Bite a totally engrossing book, I was not able to put it down, page after page I found delight, love, understanding, well that is until the bad bad Vamp started being really bad. But seeing someone love another person so much that they would do anything to protect them, well that had me going, then well there was more and for a while I thought it was the end of a beautiful love story that spanned not only time but, spanned Italy and California. Won't divulge how it ended, but I did shed a few tears after screaming but Sharon Hamilton did not let me down, she took me on amazing trip that I loved, look forward to reading another Vampire book of hers."

"An excellent paranormal romance that was exciting, romantic, entertaining and very satisfying to read. It had me anticipating what would happen next many times over, so much so I could not put it down and even finished it up in a day. The vampires in this book were different from your average vampire, but I enjoy different variations and changes to the same old stuff. It made for a more unpredictable read and more adventurous to explore! Vampire lovers, any paranormal readers and even those who love the romance genre will enjoy Honeymoon Bite."

"This is the first non-Seal book of this author's I have read and I loved it. There is a cast-like hierarchy in this vampire community with humans at the very bottom and Golden vampires at the top. Lionel is a dark vampire who are servants of the Goldens. Phoebe is a Golden who has not decided if she will remain human or accept the turning to become a vampire. Either way she and Lionel can never be together since it is forbidden.

I enjoyed this story and I am looking forward to the next installment."

"A hauntingly romantic read. Old love lost and new love found. Family, heart, intrigue and vampires. Grabbed my attention and couldn't put down. Would definitely recommend."

## PRAISE FOR THE
## SEAL BROTHERHOOD SERIES

"Fans of Navy SEAL romance, I found a new author to feed your addiction. Finely written and loaded delicious with moments, Sharon Hamilton's storytelling satisfies like a thick bar of chocolate." —Marliss Melton, bestselling author of the *Team Twelve* Navy SEALs series

"Sharon Hamilton does an EXCELLENT job of fitting all the characters into a brotherhood of SEALS that may not be real but sure makes you feel that you have entered the circle and security of their world. The stories intertwine with each book before…and each book after and THAT is what makes Sharon Hamilton's SEAL Brotherhood Series so very interesting. You won't want to put down ANY of her books and they will keep you reading into the night when you should be sleeping. Start with this book…and you will not want to stop until you've read the whole series and then…you will be waiting for Sharon to write the next one." (5 Star Review)

"Kyle and Christy explode all over the pages in this first book, *[Accidental SEAL],* in a whole new series of SEALs. If the twist and turns don't get your heart jumping, then maybe the suspense will. This is a must read for those that are looking for love and adventure with a little sloppy love thrown in for good measure." (5 Star Review)

## PRAISE FOR THE
## BAD BOYS OF SEAL TEAM 3 SERIES

"I love reading this series! Once you start these books, you can hardly put them down. The mix of romance and suspense keeps you turning the pages one right after another! Can't wait until the next book!" (5 Star Review)

"I love all of Sharon's Seal books, but *[SEAL's Code]* may just be her best to date. Danny and Luci's journey is filled with a wonderful insight into the Native American life. It is a love story that will fill you with warmth and contentment. You will enjoy Danny's journey to become a SEAL and his reasons for it. Good job Sharon!" (5 Star Review)

## PRAISE FOR THE
## BAND OF BACHELORS SERIES

"*[Lucas]* was the first book in the Band of Bachelors series and it was a phenomenal start. I loved how we got to see the other SEALs we all love and we got a look at Lucas and Marcy. They had an instant attraction, and their love was very intense. This book had it all, suspense, steamy romance, humor, everything you want in a riveting, outstanding read. I can't wait to read the next book in this series." (5 Star Review)

## PRAISE FOR THE
## TRUE BLUE SEALS SERIES

"Keep the tissues box nearby as you read *True Blue SEALs: Zak* by Sharon Hamilton. I imagine more than I wish to that the circumstances surrounding Zak and Amy are all too real for returning military personnel and their families. Ms. Hamilton has put us right in the middle of struggles and successes that these two high school sweethearts endure. I have read several of Sharon Hamilton's military romances but will say this is the most emotionally intense of the ones that I have read. This is a well-written, realistic story with authentic characters that will have you rooting for them and proud of those who serve to keep us safe. This is an author who writes amazing stories that you love and cry with the characters. Fans of Jessica Scott and Marliss Melton will want to add Sharon Hamilton to their list of realistic military romance writers." (5 Star Review)

Made in the USA
Columbia, SC
29 October 2023